THE STRANGE WORLD
OF JUDITH MERRIL

In the dozen years since her first published
story, Judith Merril has won a very special
place in fiction. Her stories of today and
the near and far future focus unerringly on the
people in them—not the Gimmick or the Gadget.

Now, from that dozen years of work, author and
critic Theodore Sturgeon has selected seven
of her best—stories of people in love and hate,
stories of real men and women living in worlds
that only Judith Merril could imagine—worlds

OUT OF BOUNDS

OUT OF BOUNDS

Seven stories by
Judith Merril
With an introduction by
Theodore Sturgeon

PYRAMID BOOKS ▲ NEW YORK

OUT OF BOUNDS

A Pyramid Book

First printing, April 1960
Second printing, February 1963

*This book is fiction. No resemblance is intended between
any character herein and any person, living or dead; any
such resemblance is purely coincidental.*

Acknowledgments

"That Only a Mother," copyright 1948, by Street &
Smith, Inc.; originally appeared in *Astounding Science
Fiction*, June 1948

"Peeping Tom," copyright 1954, by Standard Magazines;
originally appeared in *Startling Stories*, Spring 1954

"The Lady Was a Tramp," copyright 1957, by Fantasy
Press; originally appeared in *Venture Science Fiction*,
July 1957

"Whoever You Are," copyright 1952, by Standard Magazines; originally appeared in *Startling Stories*, December 1952

"Connection Completed," copyright 1954, by Standard
Magazines; originally appeared in *Universe*, Summer
1954

"Dead Center," copyright 1954, by Fantasy Press; originally appeared in *The Magazine of Fantasy and
Science Fiction*, November 1954

"Death Cannot Wither," copyright 1958, by Fantasy
Press; originally appeared in *The Magazine of Fantasy and Science Fiction*, February 1959

Pyramid Books *are published by Pyramid Publications, Inc.,
444 Madison Avenue, New York 22, New York, U.S.A.*

CONTENTS

Introduction: *Theodore Sturgeon*   7

That Only a Mother   11

Peeping Tom   22

The Lady Was a Tramp   47

Whoever You Are   67

Connection Completed   96

Dead Center   108

Death Cannot Wither   137

INTRODUCTION

IT SEEMS there was a travelling salesman. There really was. He was seedy and he was sad, and he travelled from door to door in Chelsea—that section of the lower West Side of New York lying between the more famous Village and the more infamous Hell's Kitchen. If he ever sold his wares I do not know, except as I may here bear witness he sold nothing to me; he did, however, carry news of me, a writer barely begun, to the ears of Miss Merril, a writer barely beginning.

There followed a letter and a meeting. Her letter contained some flattery of a nature quite overwhelming until tempered by the meeting, at which I was quickly made aware of the fact that nobody who had actually sold a story to a magazine—even a minor story to a minor magazine—could escape her awe. In other words, the status Writer was of greater importance to her than any writer. Even me.

At the time she had not yet sold a word, and her chant, her theme, was, "I want to be a Writer!" and the anomaly in this was that she was one, and that anyone in the scrivening trade who ever talked to her knew immediately that she was; that she was a writer in every respect, from top to toe to inside to out, who could write and would write and must write if it was on wet cardboard in the pouring rain with a pointed stick; and *she didn't know it!*

Telling her did no good, because she didn't believe it. Yet—what is a writer, anyway? What elements produce that subspecies? Why, only those she had, and has in such full measure; and I shall enumerate:

A respect for the craft. One way to restate this is to say that the pen is mightier than the sword; and the fair extrapolation of *that*, these nuclear days, is that the word is mightier than the bomb—it is, indeed, truly the ultimate weapon, and the writer writes respectfully, knowing this.

Something to say. This is what the Writer does with what he has, and the more he respects what he has, the more significant is what he does.

Empathy. Some say a writer has to be interested in people. Some go further and say he has to love people. But a Writer must be able to see out through other people's eyes and feel with their fingertips.

Humility. One expression of this is "It isn't finished yet," in the sense that anything alive is mutable in every fibre; changing, growing; so that a Writer's writing has about it the quality of life—not harvested and handed you dewy and fresh, and you'd better gobble it before it goes bad, but able, rather, to live as you live, grow as you grow —to bring you fruits of sight and insight to the degree that the soil and climate of You can nurture it.

Finally, if the writer is to write fiction, there must be the acquisition of the techniques of fiction, and the most profound understanding that a story about an Idea or a Thing might be a tract or an article or an anecdote, but unless and until it is about people, it is not fiction.

From the very beginning—and even before that!—Judith Merril was a Writer. It may be, however, that she marks the very beginning with THAT ONLY A MOTHER (humility at work, you see.) And I would like to say a special few words about this extra-special story.

I have gone over the contents of this collection (incredibly, her first) in its pre-natal form of galleys and tearsheets, and I wish you could see it that way too. For every story shows work and more work—touch here, polish there, rewrite, re-proportion—all the effort which means only that this author regards these stories as alive and growing, even as she has lived and grown since she first wrote them, and as, therefore, they must live and grow with you. But in one special case I have requested that the story run just as it first appeared, so that, along with the story, you may read the author.

THAT ONLY A MOTHER is a story that only a

mother could have written. What I especially wish to point out is the so-called "dating" of this story. It takes place in 1953. But what a 1953! We take our morning newspaper out of a home facsimile gadget. We travel up to the seventeenth floor in a Rolavator, whatever that is, and, what with nuclear warfare and unbridled research, there is a rising incidence of mutations; infanticide—most often by the fathers—is a rising tide. All of this is ridiculous, of course: what the lit'ry journals are pleased to dismiss as "mere" science fiction. (Oddly enough, if we now said—for this edition—'63 or '83, we would feel that the story was more realistic, or at least less dated. "Dated," you know, means beneath consideration.)

It is important, however, not to accept such trivial reasons for dismissing such a story. For this is a 'world of if' story; it is science-fiction functioning, not in its 'might-happen' voice, but in its even more potent 'might-have-happened' one. We really might have had such a '53 —rolavators and all, for war does strange swift things to the appointments of living—but for the power of the word.

Now go back and watch the Writer writing this story. Hiroshima is less than two years ago; this is the time of One World or None and the Soviet scuttling of the Baruch Plan in the United Nations. I am not, on behalf of this remarkable story, suggesting that it was the word that turned aside the '53 it describes; I do submit that the Writer writes it because she has something to say; that her deep conviction is that to say it in powerful terms— human terms—is what she can do about what is happening around her; and that she feels it is worth doing with all that she knows best and feels most deeply—motherhood, childbirth, love, fear, and a uniquely vivid female-ness.

Read the story and the Writer with these things in mind, and then contemplate the fact that this was Judith Merril's very first sale, and perhaps you'll understand why those of us who knew her, as it were, before she was born, knew that she was a Writer.

What else is in store for you? There's PEEPING TOM,

one of the many stories which result from the author's profound and informative interest in the peripheral powers of the mind—and a bit about the powers of the body as well, all tucked in with a neat twist which demonstrates (if I may reach in the box for another metaphor) that a good laugh must of necessity have teeth in it.

And there's THE LADY WAS A TRAMP. Here's technological science fiction as be-gadgetted as a radar parts warehouse, plotted like a problem in astronautics—and all, all about people; but I mean in the saltiest possible terms.

And WHOEVER YOU ARE—again the intricately plotted future world—space ships, alien invasion—war, weapons, death—and oh, the most poignant message! Did a science fiction story ever make you cry? No?

Then, CONNECTION COMPLETED—a brief and very real adventure in the here-and-now—a couple of uncertain and wonderstruck people who know something about each other which they can't be sure of.

And if you've never read DEAD CENTER—I envy you the first contact. This was the story Martha Foley chose for one of her annual "best" anthologies. You'll see why.

Finally, DEATH CANNOT WITHER. This is the only true "fantasy" story in the book, in the sense that one of the characters is a ghost. Ghost or not, he's real —by any test you can think of—and this concluding tale has as important things to say about life and love, and says them as brilliantly, as the others.

The whole thing only goes to show, in other words, that Judith Merril, editor, anthologist, teacher, parent, is a Writer. Which, of course, I knew all along.

Theodore Sturgeon
Woodstock, New York
January, 1960

THAT ONLY A MOTHER

MARGARET
reached over to the other side of the bed where Hank
should have been. Her hand patted the empty pillow, and
then she came altogether awake, wondering that the old
habit should remain after so many months. She tried to
curl up, cat-style, to hoard her own warmth, found she
couldn't do it any more, and climbed out of bed with a
pleased awareness of her increasingly clumsy bulkiness.

Morning motions were automatic. On the way through
the kitchenette, she pressed the button that would start
breakfast cooking—the doctor had said to eat as much
breakfast as she could—and tore the paper out of the
facsimile machine. She folded the long sheet carefully to
the "National News" section, and propped it on the
bathroom shelf to scan while she brushed her teeth.

No accidents. No direct hits. At least none that had
been officially released for publication. *Now, Maggie,
don't get started on that. No accidents. No hits. Take the
nice newspaper's word for it.*

The three clear chimes from the kitchen announced that
breakfast was ready. She set a bright napkin and cheerful colored dishes on the table in a futile attempt to ap-
peal to a faulty morning appetite. Then when there was
nothing more to prepare, she went for the mail, allowing
herself the full pleasure of prolonged anticipation, because today there would surely be a letter.

There was. There was. Two bills and a worried note
from her mother: "Darling, why didn't you write and tell

11

me sooner? I'm thrilled, of course, but, well one hates to mention these things, but are you certain the doctor was right? Hank's been around all that uranium or thorium or whatever it is all these years, and I know you say he's a designer, not a technician, and he doesn't get near anything that might be dangerous, but you know he used to, back at Oak Ridge. Don't you think . . . well, of course, I'm just being a foolish old woman, and I don't want you to get upset. You know much more about it than I do, and I'm sure your doctor was right. He should know . . ."

Margaret made a face over the excellent coffee, and caught herself refolding the paper to the medical news.

Stop it, Maggie, stop it! The radiologist said Hank's job couldn't have exposed him. And the bombed area we drove past . . . No, no. Stop it, now! Read the social notes or the recipes, Maggie girl.

A well-known geneticist, in the medical news, said that it was possible to tell with absolute certainty, at five months, whether the child would be normal, or at least whether the mutation was likely to produce anything freakish. The worst cases, at any rate, could be prevented. Minor mutations, of course, displacements in facial features or changes in brain structure could not be detected. And there had been some cases recently of normal embryos with atrophied limbs that did not develop beyond the seventh or eighth month. But, the doctor concluded cheerfully, the worst cases could now be predicted and prevented.

"Predicted and prevented." We predicted it, didn't we? Hank and the others, they predicted it. But we didn't prevent it. We could have stopped it in '46 and '47. Now . . .

Margaret decided against the breakfast. Coffee had been enough for her in the morning for ten years; it would have to do for today. She buttoned herself into the interminable folds of material that, the salesgirl had assured her, was the only comfortable thing to wear during the last few months. With a surge of pure pleasure, the letter and newspaper forgotten, she realized she was on the next to the last button. It wouldn't be long now.

The city in the early morning had always been a special kind of excitement for her. Last night it had rained, and the sidewalks were still damp-gray instead of dusty. The air smelled the fresher, to a city-bred woman, for the occasional pungency of acrid factory smoke. She walked the six blocks to work, watching the lights go out in the all-night hamburger joints, where the plate-glass walls were already catching the sun, and the lights go on in the dim interiors of cigar stores and dry-cleaning establishments.

The office was in a new Government building. In the rolovator, on the way up, she felt, as always, like a frankfurter roll in the ascending half of an old-style rotary toasting machine. She abandoned the air-foam cushioning gratefully at the fourteenth floor, and settled down behind her desk, at the rear of a long row of identical desks.

Each morning the pile of papers that greeted her was a little higher. These were, as everyone knew, the decisive months. The war might be won or lost on these calculations as well as any others. The manpower office had switched her here when her old expediter's job got to be too strenuous. The computer was easy to operate, and the work was absorbing, if not as exciting as the old job. But you didn't just stop working these days. Everyone who could do anything at all was needed.

And—she remembered the interview with the psychologist—*I'm probably the unstable type. Wonder what sort of neurosis I'd get sitting home reading that sensational paper . . .*

She plunged into the work without pursuing the thought.

February 18.

Hank darling,

Just a note—from the hospital, no less. I had a dizzy spell at work, and the doctor took it to heart. Blessed if I know what I'll do with myself lying in bed for weeks, just waiting—but Dr. Boyer seems to think it may not be so long.

There are too many newspapers around here. More infanticides all the time, and they can't seem to get a jury to convict any of them. It's the fathers who do it. Lucky thing you're not around, in case—

Oh, darling, that wasn't a very funny joke, was it? Write as often as you can, will you? I have too much time to think. But there really isn't anything wrong, and nothing to worry about.

Write often, and remember I love you.

Maggie.

SPECIAL SERVICE TELEGRAM—February 21, 1953
   22:04   LK37G
From: Tech. Lieut. H. Marvell
          X47-016   GCNY
                     To: Mrs. H. Marvell
                         Women's Hospital
                         New York City
HAD DOCTOR'S GRAM STOP WILL ARRIVE FOUR OH TEN STOP SHORT LEAVE STOP YOU DID IT MAGGIE STOP LOVE HANK

February 25

Hank dear,

So you didn't see the baby either? You'd think a place this size would at least have visiplates on the incubators, so the fathers could get a look, even if the poor benighted mommas can't. They tell me I won't see her for another week, or maybe more—but of course, mother always warned me if I didn't slow my pace, I'd probably even have my babies too fast. Why must she always be right?

Did you meet that battle-ax of a nurse they put on here? I imagine they save her for people who've already had theirs, and don't let her get too near the prospectives— but a woman like that simply shouldn't be allowed in a maternity ward. She's obsessed with mutations, can't seem to talk about anything else. Oh, well, ours is all right even if it was in an unholy hurry.

I'm tired. They warned me not to sit up so soon, but I had to write you. All my love, darling,

Maggie.

February 29.

Darling,

I finally got to see her! It's all true, what they say about new babies and the face that only a mother could love—but it's all there, darling, eyes, ears, and noses—no, only one!—all in the right places. We're so lucky, Hank.

I'm afraid I've been a rambunctious patient. I kept telling that hatchet-faced female with the mutation mania that I wanted to see the baby. Finally the doctor came in to "explain" everything to me, and talked a lot of nonsense, most of which I'm sure no one could have understood, any more than I did. The only thing I got out of it was that she didn't actually have to stay in the incubator; they just thought it was "wiser."

I think I got a little hysterical at that point. Guess I was more worried than I was willing to admit, but I threw a small fit about it. The whole business wound up with one of those hushed medical conferences outside the door, and finally the Woman in White said: "Well, we might as well. Maybe it'll work out better that way."

I'd heard about the way doctors and nurses in these places develop a God complex, and believe me it is as true figuratively as it is literally that a mother hasn't got a leg to stand on around here

I am awfully weak, still. I'll write again soon. Love,

Maggie

March 8.

Dearest Hank,

Well the nurse was wrong if she told you that. She's an idiot anyhow. It's a girl. It's easier to tell with babies than with cats, and I know. How about Henrietta?

I'm home again, and busier than a betatron. They got everything mixed up at the hospital, and I had to teach myself how to bathe her and do just about everything else. She's getting prettier, too. When can you get a leave, a real leave?

Love,
Maggie.

May 26.

Hank dear,

You should see her now—and you shall. I'm sending along a reel of color movie. My mother sent her those nighties with drawstrings all over. I put one on, and right now she looks like a snow-white potato sack with that beautiful, beautiful flower-face blooming on top. Is that me talking? Am I a doting mother? But wait till you see her!

July 10.

. . . Believe it or not, as you like, but your daughter can talk, and I don't mean baby talk. Alice discovered it—she's a dental assistant in the WACs, you know—and when she heard the baby giving out what I thought was a string of gibberish, she said the kid knew words and sentences, but couldn't say them clearly because she has no teeth yet. I'm taking her to a speech specialist.

September 13.

. . . We have a prodigy for real! Now that all her front teeth are in, her speech is perfectly clear and—a new talent now—she can sing! I mean really carry a tune! At seven months! Darling my world would be perfect if you could only get home.

November 19

. . . at last. The little goon was so busy being clever, it took her all this time to learn to crawl. The doctor says development in these cases is always erratic . .

SPECIAL SERVICE TELEGRAM

December 1, 1953
08:47   LK59F

From: Tech. Lieut. H. Marvell
X47-016   GCNY

To: Mrs. H. Marvell
Apt. K-17
504 E. 19 St.
N.Y., N.Y

WEEK'S LEAVE STARTS TOMORROW STOP
WILL ARRIVE AIRPORT TEN OH FIVE STOP
DON'T MEET ME STOP LOVE LOVE LOVE
HANK

Margaret let the water run out of the bathinette until
only a few inches were left, and then loosed her hold on
the wriggling baby.

"I think it was better when you were retarded, young
woman," she informed her daughter happily. "You can't
crawl in a bathinette, you know."

"Then why can't I go in the bathtub?" Margaret was
used to her child's volubility by now, but every now and
then it caught her unawares. She swooped the resistant
mass of pink flesh into a towel, and began to rub.

"Because you're too little, and your head is very soft,
and bathtubs are very hard."

"Oh. Then when can I go in the bathtub?"

"When the outside of your head is as hard as the inside, brainchild." She reached toward a pile of fresh cloth-
ing. "I cannot understand," she added, pinning a square
of cloth through the nightgown, "why a child of your
intelligence can't learn to keep a diaper on the way other
babies do. They've been used for centuries, you know, with
perfectly satisfactory results."

The child disdained to reply; she had heard it too often.
She waited patiently until she had been tucked, clean
and sweet-smelling, into a white-painted crib. Then she
favored her mother with a smile that inevitably made
Margaret think of the first golden edge of the sun bursting into a rosy pre-dawn. She remembered Hank's reaction
to the color pictures of his beautiful daughter, and with
the thought, realized how late it was.

"Go to sleep, puss. When you wake up, you know,
your Daddy will be here."

"Why?" asked the four-year-old mind, waging a losing
battle to keep the ten-month-old body awake.

Margaret went into the kitchenette and set the timer
for the roast. She examined the table, and got her clothes
from the closet, new dress, new shoes, new slip, new every-

thing, bought weeks before and saved for the day Hank's telegram came. She stopped to pull a paper from the facsimile and, with clothes and news, went into the bathroom, and lowered herself gingerly into the steaming luxury of a scented tub.

She glanced through the paper with indifferent interest. Today at least there was no need to read the national news. There was an article by a geneticist. The same geneticist. Mutations, he said, were increasing disproportionately. It was too soon for recessives; even the first mutants, born near Hiroshima and Nagasaki in 1946 and 1947 were not old enough yet to breed. *But my body's all right.* Apparently, there was some degree of free radiation from atomic explosions causing the trouble. *My baby's fine. Precocious, but normal.* If more attention had been paid to the first Japanese mutations, he said . . .

There was that little notice in the paper in the spring of '47. That was when Hank quit at Oak Ridge. "Only two or three per cent of those guilty of infanticide are being caught and punished in Japan today . . ." But MY BABY'S all right.

She was dressed, combed, and ready to the last light brush-on of lip paste, when the door chime sounded. She dashed for the door, and heard, for the first time in eighteen months the almost-forgotten sound of a key turning in the lock before the chime had quite died away.

"Hank!"

"Maggie!"

And then there was nothing to say. So many days, so many months, of small news piling up, so many things to tell him, and now she just stood there, staring at a khaki uniform and a stranger's pale face. She traced the features with the finger of memory. The same high-bridged nose, wide-set eyes, fine feathery brows; the same long jaw, the hair a little farther back now on the high forehead, the same tilted curve to his mouth. Pale . . . Of course, he'd been underground all this time. And strange, stranger because of lost familiarity than any newcomer's face could be.

She had time to think all that before his hand reached

out to touch her, and spanned the gap of eighteen months. Now, again, there was nothing to say, because there was no need. They were together, and for the moment that was enough.

"Where's the baby?"

"Sleeping. She'll be up any minute."

No urgency. Their voice were as casual as though it were a daily exchange, as though war and sepration did not exist. Margaret picked up the coat he'd thrown on the chair near the door, and hung it carefully in the hall closet. She went to check the roast, leaving him to wander through the rooms by himself, remembering and coming back. She found him, finally, standing over the baby's crib.

She couldn't see his face, but she had no need to.

"I think we can wake her just this once." Margaret pulled the covers down, and lifted the white bundle from the bed. Sleepy lids pulled back heavily from smoky brown eyes.

"Hello." Hank's voice was tentative.

"Hello." The baby's assurance was more pronounced.

He had heard about it, of course, but that wasn't the same as hearing it. He turned eagerly to Margaret. "She really can—?"

"Of course she can, darling. But what's more important, she can even do nice normal things like other babies do, even stupid ones. Watch her crawl!" Margaret set the baby on the big bed.

For a moment young Henrietta lay and eyed her parents dubiously.

"Crawl?" she asked.

"That's the idea. Your Daddy is new around here, you know. He wants to see you show off."

"Then put me on my tummy."

"Oh, of course." Margaret obligingly rolled the baby over.

"What's the matter?" Hank's voice was still casual, but an undercurrent in it began to charge the air of the room. "I thought they turned over first."

"This baby," Margaret would not notice the tension "This baby does things when she wants to."

This baby's father watched with softening eyes while the head advanced and the body hunched up, propelling itself across the bed.

"Why the little rascal," he burst into relieved laughter. "She looks like one of those potato-sack racers they used to have on picnics. Got her arms pulled out of the sleeves already." He reached over and grabbed the knot at the bottom of the long nightie.

"I'll do it, darling." Margaret tried to get there first.

"Don't be silly, Maggie. This may be your first baby, but I had five kid brothers." He laughed her away, and reached with his other hand for the string that closed one sleeve. He opened the sleeve bow, and groped for an arm.

"The way you wiggle," he addressed his child sternly, as his hand touched a moving knob of flesh at the shoulder, "anyone might think you were a worm, using your tummy to crawl on, instead of your hands and feet."

Margaret stood and watched, smiling. "Wait till you hear her sing, darling—"

His right hand traveled down from the shoulder to where he thought an arm would be, traveled down, and straight down, over firm small muscles that writhed in an attempt to move against the pressure of his hand. He let his fingers drift up again to the shoulder. With infinite care, he opened the knot at the bottom of the nightgown. His wife was standing by the bed, saying: "She can do 'Jingle Bells,' and—"

His left hand felt along the soft knitted fabric of the gown, up towards the diaper that folded, flat and smooth, across the bottom end of his child. No wrinkles. No kicking. No . . .

"Maggie." He tried to pull his hands from the neat fold in the diaper, from the wriggling body. "Maggie." His throat was dry; words came hard, low and grating. He spoke very slowly, thinking the sound of each word to make himself say it. His head was spinning, but he had to know before he let it go. "Maggie, why . . . didn't you . . . tell me?"

"Tell you what, darling?" Margaret's poise was the immemorial patience of woman confronted with man's childish impetuosity. Her sudden laugh sounded fantastically easy and natural in that room; it was all clear to her now. "Is she wet? I didn't know."

She didn't know. His hands, beyond control, ran up and down the soft-skinned baby body, the sinuous, limbless body. *Oh God dear God*—his head shook and his muscles contracted, in a bitter spasm of hysteria. His fingers tightened on his child—*Oh God, she didn't know.*

PEEPING
TOM

YOU TAKE a boy like Tommy Bender—a nice American boy, well-brought-up in a nice, average, middle-class family; chock-full of vitamins, manners and baseball statistics; clean-shaven, soft-spoken, and respectful to women and his elders. You take a boy like that, fit him out with a uniform, teach him to operate the most modern means of manslaughter, reward him with a bright gold bar, and send him out to an exotic eastern land to prove his manhood and his patriotism.

You take a kid like that. Send him into combat in a steaming jungle inferno; teach him to sweat and swear with conviction; then wait till he makes just one wrong move, pick him out of the pool of drying blood, beat off the flies, and settle him safely on a hospital cot in an ill-equipped base behind the lines, cut off from everyone and everywhere, except the little native village nearby. Let him rest and rot there for a while. Then bring him home, and pin a medal on him, and give him his civvies and a pension to go with his limp. You take a boy like Tommy Bender, and do all that to him, you won't expect him to be quite the same nice, apple-cheeked youngster afterwards.

He wasn't.

When Tommy Bender came home, he was firmly disillusioned and grimly determined. He knew what he wanted out of life, had practically no hope of getting it, and didn't much care how he went about getting the next best things. And in a remarkably short time, he made it clear to his erstwhile friends and neighbors that he was almost certain to get anything he went after. He made money; he made love; he made enemies. Eventually, he made enough of a success so that the enemies could be as thoroughly ignored as yesterday's woman. The money, and the things it bought for him, he took good care of.

For almost five years after he came home, Tommy Bender continued to build a career and ruin reputations. People tried to understand what had happened to him; but they didn't really.

Then, abruptly, something happened to change Tommy. His business associates noticed it first; his family afterwards. The girls he was seeing at the time were the last to know, because he'd always been undependable with them, and not hearing from him for two or three weeks wasn't unusual.

What happened was a girl. Her name was Candace, and when she was married to Tommy, seven weeks after her arrival, the papers carried the whole romantic story. It was she who had nursed him back to health in that remote village on the edge of the jungle years ago. He'd been in love with her then, but she'd turned him down.

That last part wasn't in the news story of course, but it got around town just as fast as the paper did. Tommy's bitterness, it seemed, was due to his long-frustrated love. And anyone could see how he'd changed since Candace came back to him. His employees, his debtors, his old friends and discarded women, his nervous mother and his angry brother all sighed with relief and decided everything was going to be all right now. At last they really understood.

But they didn't. They didn't, for instance, understand what happened to Tommy Bender in that God-forsaken little town where he'd spent two months on crutches, waiting for his leg to heal enough to travel home.

It was hot and sticky in the shack. The mattress was lumpy. His leg itched to the very fringes of madness, and the man on his right had an erratically syncopated snore

that took him past the raveled edge straight to insanity.
All he needed to make the torture complete was the guy
on his left—and the nurse.

The nurse was young and round and lithe, and she wore
battle fatigues: slacks, and a khaki shirt that was always
draped against her high, full breasts in the damp heat.
Her hair, dark blonde or light brown, was just long enough
to be pinned back in a tiny bun, and just short enough
so wisps of it were always escaping to curl around her
ears or over her forehead.

When she bent over him to do any of the small humiliating services he needed done for him, he could see tiny
beads of sweat on her upper lip, and that somehow was
always the one little touch too much.

So that after she moved on to the next bed, and beyond
it, it would be torture to have Dake, the guy on the left,
turn toward him and start describing, graphically, what
he would do if he could just get his remaining arm out of
the cast for fifteen minutes some day.

You see Tommy Bender was still a nice young man
then—after the combat, and the wound, and the flies, and
the rough hospitalization.

Dake was nothing of the sort. He'd been around, and he
knew exactly what value he placed on a woman. And he
enjoyed talking about it.

Tommy listened because there was no way not to, and
he wriggled and sweated and suffered, and the itch in his
leg got worse, and the stench from the garbage pile outside became unbearable. It went on that way, hour after
hour and day after day, punctuated only by the morning visit from the medic, who would stop and look
him over, and shake a weary, discouraged head, and then
go on to the next man.

The leg was a long time healing. It was better after
Dake left, and was replaced with a quietly dying man
who'd got it in the belly. After him, there was a nice
young Negro soldier, somewhat embarrassed about being
in sick bay with nothing more dramatic than appendicitis.
But at least, now, Tommy could keep his thoughts and
dreams about Candace to himself, untarnished.

Then one day, when it had begun to seem as if nothing would ever change again in his life, except the occupants of the beds on either side of him, something happened to break the monotony of discomfort and despair. The medic stopped a little longer than usual in front of Tommy's cot, studied the neat chart Candy was always filling in, and furrowed his brow with concern. Then he muttered something to Candace, and she looked worried too. After that, they both turned and looked at Tommy as if they were seeing him for the first time, and Candy smiled, and the doctor frowned a little deeper.

"Well, young man," he said, "We're going to let you get up."

"Thanks, doc," Tommy said, talking like a GI was supposed to. "What should I do with the leg? Leave it in bed?"

"Ha, ha," the doctor laughed. Just like that. "Good to see you haven't lost your spirit." Then he moved on to the next bed, and Tommy lay there wondering. What would he do with the leg?

That afternoon, they came for him with a stretcher, and took him to the surgery shack, and cut off the cast. They all stood around, five or six of them, looking at it and shaking their heads and agreeing it was pretty bad. Then they put a new cast on, a little less bulky than the first one, and handed him a pair of crutches, and said: "Okay, boy, you're on your own."

An orderly showed him how to use them, and helped him get back to his own bed. The next day he practiced up a little, and by the day after that, he could really get around.

It made a difference.

Tommy Bender was a nice normal American boy, with all the usual impulses. He had been weeks on end in the jungle, and further weeks on his back in the cot. It was not strange that he should show a distinct tendency to follow Candy about from place to place, now he was on his feet again.

The pursuit was not so much hopeful as it was instinctive. He never, quite, made any direct advance to her. He ran little errands, and helped in every way he could, as soon as he was sufficiently adept in the handling of his crutches. She was certainly not ill-pleased by his devotion, but neither, he knew, was she inclined to any sort of romantic attachment to him.

Once or twice, acting on private advice from the more experienced ambulant patients, he made tentative approaches to some of the other nurses, but met always the same kindly advice that they felt chasing nurses would not be good for his leg. He accepted his rebuffs in good part, as a nice boy will, and continued to trail around after Candy.

It was she, quite inadvertently, who led him to a piece of good fortune. He saw her leave the base one early evening, laden with packages, and traveling on foot. Alone. For a GI, these phenomena might not have been unusual. For a nurse to depart in this manner was extraordinary, and Candace slipped out so quietly that Tommy felt certain no one but himself was aware of it.

He hesitated about following at first; then he started worrying about her, threw social caution to the winds, and went swinging down the narrow road behind her, till she heard him coming and turned to look, then to wait.

She was irritated at first; then, abruptly, she seemed to change her mind.

"All right, come along," she said. "It's just a visit I'm going to pay. You can't come in with me, but you can wait if you want to, and walk me back again."

He couldn't have been more pleased. Or curious.

Their walk took them directly into the native village, where Candace seemed to become confused. She led Tommy and his crutches up and down a number of dirty streets and evil-looking alleys before she located the small earthen hut she was looking for, with a wide stripe of blue clay over its door.

While they searched for the place, she explained nervously to Tommy that she was fulfilling a mission for a dead soldier, who had, in a period of false recovery just before the end, made friends with an old man of this vil-

lage. The dying GI had entrusted her with messages and
gifts for his friend—most notably a sealed envelope and
his last month's cigarette ration. That had been three
weeks ago, and she'd spent the time since working up her
courage to make the trip. Now, she confessed, she was
more than glad Tommy had come along.

When they found the hut at last, they found a com-
paratively clean old man sitting cross-legged by the doorway, completely enveloped in a long gray robe with a hood
thrown back off his shaven head. There was a begging bowl
at his side, and Tommy suggested that Candace might do
best just to leave her offerings in the bowl. But when she
bent down to do so, the old man raised his head and
smiled at her.

"You are a friend of my friend, Karl?" he asked in astonishingly good English.

"Why . . . yes," she fumbled. "Yes. Karl Larsen. He
said to bring you these. . . ."

"I thank you. You were most kind to come so soon."
He stood up, and added, just to her, ignoring Tommy.
"Will you come inside and drink tea with me, and speak
with me of his death?"

"Why, I—" Suddenly she too smiled, apparently quite
at ease once more. "Yes, I'd be glad to. Thank you.
Tommy," she added, "would you mind waiting for me?
I . . . I'd appreciate having someone to walk back with.
It won't be long. Maybe—" she looked at the old man
who was smiling, waiting—"maybe half an hour," she
finished.

"A little more or less perhaps," he said, in his startlingly
clear American diction. "Perhaps your friend would enjoy
looking about our small village meanwhile, and you two
can meet again here in front of my door?"

"Why, sure," Tommy said, but he wasn't sure at all.
Because as he started to say it, he had no intention of
moving away from that door at all while Candy was inside. He'd stay right there, within earshot. But by the
time the second word was forming in his mouth, he had
a sudden clear image of what he'd be doing during that
time.

And he was right.

No sooner had Candy passed under the blue-topped doorway than a small boy appeared at Tommy's other elbow. The youngster's English was in no way comparable to that of the old man. He knew just two words, but they were sufficient. The first was: "Youguhcigarreh?" The second:: "Iguhsisseh."

Tommy dug in his pockets, came out with a half-full pack, registered the boy's look of approval, and swung his crutches into action. He followed his young friend up and down several of the twisty village alleys, and out along a footpath into the forest. Just about the time he was beginning to get worried, they came out into a small clearing, and a moment later "Sisseh" emerged from behind a tree at the far edge.

She was disconcertingly young, but also unexpectedly attractive: smooth-skinned, graceful, and roundly shaped. . . .

Somewhat later when he found his way back to the blue-topped door in the village, Candy was already waiting for him, looking thoughtful and a little sad. She ~med to be no more in the mood for conversation than w. Tommy himself, and they walked back to the base in almost complete silence. Though he noted once or twice that her quiet mood was dictated by less happy considerations than his own, Tommy's ease of mind and body was too great at that moment to encourage much concern for even so desirable a symbol of American womanhood as the beautiful nurse, Candace.

Not that his devotion to her lessened. He dreamed of her still, but the dreams were more pleasantly romantic, and less distressingly carnal. And on those occasions when he found his thoughts of her verging once more toward the improper, he would wander off to the little village and regain what he felt was a more natural and suitable attitude toward life and love in general.

Then, inevitably, there came one such day when his young procurer was nowhere to be found. Tommy went out to the clearing where Sisseh usually met them, but it was quiet, empty and deserted. Back in the village again, he wandered aimlessly up and down narrow twisting streets, till he found himself passing the blue-topped doorway of the old man whose friendship with a dead GI had started the whole chain of events in motion.

"Good morning, sir," the old man said, and Tommy stopped politely to return the greeting.

"You are looking for your young friend?"

Tommy nodded, and hoped the warmth he could feel on his face didn't show. Small-town gossip, apparently, was much the same in one part of the world as in another.

"I think he will be busy for some time yet," the old man volunteered. "Perhaps another hour . . . his mother required his services for an errand to another village."

"Well, thanks," Tommy said. "Guess I'll come back this afternoon or something. Thanks a lot."

"You may wait here with me if you like. You are most welcome," the old man said hastily. "Perhaps you would care to come into my home and drink tea with me?"

Tommy's manners were good. He had been taught to be respectful to his elders, even to the old colored man who came to clip the hedges. And he knew that an invitation to tea can never be refus~¹ ~vithout excellent good reason. He had no such reason, anu he did have a warm interest in seeing his dusky beauty just as soon as possible. He therefore overcame a natural reluctance to become a visitor in one of the (doubtless) vermin-infested native huts, thanked the old man politely, and accepted the invitation.

Those few steps, passing under the blue-topped doorway for the first time, into the earthen shack, were beyond doubt the most momentous of his young life. When he came out again, a full two hours later, there was nothing on the surface to show what had happened to him . . . except perhaps a more-than-usually thoughtful look on his face. But when Sisseh's little brother pursued him down the village street, Tommy only shook his head. And when the boy persisted, the soldier said briefly: "No got cigarettes."

The statement did not in any way express the empty-handed regret one might have expected. It was rather an impatient dismissal by a man too deeply immersed in weighty affairs to regard either the cigarettes or their value in trade as having much importance.

Not that Tommy had lost any of his vigorous interest in the pleasures of the flesh. He had simply acquired a more far-sighted point of view. He had plans for the future now, and they did not concern a native girl whose affection was exchangeable for half a pack of Camels.

Swinging along the jungle path on his crutches, Tommy was approaching a dazzling new vista of hope and ambition. The goals he had once considered quite out of reach now seemed to be just barely beyond his grasp, and he had already embarked on a course of action calculated to remedy that situation. Tommy was apprenticed to telepath.

The way it happened, the whole incredible notion seemed like a perfectly natural idea. Inside the one-room hut, the old man had introduced himself as Armod Something-or-other. (The last name was a confusion of clashing consonants and strangely inflected vowels that Tommy never quite got straight.) He then invited his young guest to make himself comfortable, and began the preparation of the tea by pouring water from a swan-necked glass bottle into a burnished copper kettle suspended by graceful chains from a wrought-iron tripod over a standard-brand hardware store Sterno stove.

The arrangement was typical of everything in the room. East met West at every point with a surprising minimum of friction, once the first impact was absorbed and the psychological dislocation adjusted.

Tommy settled down at first on a low couch, really no more than a native mat covering some woven webbing, stretched across a frame that stood a few inches off the floor on carved ivory claws. But he discovered quickly enough that it did not provide much in the way of comfort for a long-legged young man equipped with a bulky cast. An awful lot of him seemed to be stretched out over the red-and-white tile pattern linoleum that covered the center of the dirt floor . . . and he noticed, too, that his crutches had left a trail of round dust-prints on the otherwise spotless surface.

He wiped off the padded bottoms of the crutches with his clean handkerchief, and struggled rather painfully back to his feet.

The whole place was astonishingly clean. Tommy wandered around, considerably relieved at the absence of any very noticeable insect life, examining the curious contents of the room, and politely refraining from asking the many questions that came to mind.

The furnishing consisted primarily of low stools and tables, with a few shelves somehow set into the clay wall. There was one large, magnificently carved mahogany chest, which might have contained Ali Baba's fortune; and on a teakwood table in the corner, with a pad on the floor for a seat, stood a large and shiny late-model American standard typewriter.

A bookshelf near the table caught Tommy's eye, and the old man, without turning around, invited his guest to inspect it. Here again was the curious mixture of East and West: new books on philosophy, psychology, semantics, cybernetics published in England and America. Several others, though fewer, on spiritualism, psychic phenomena, and radio-esthesia. And mixed in with them, apparently at random, short squat volumes and long thin ones, lettered in unfamiliar scripts and ideographs.

On the wall over the bookshelf hung two strips of parchment, such as may be seen in many eastern homes, covered with ideograph characters brilliantly illuminated. Between them was a glass-faced black frame containing the certification of Armod's license to practice medicine in the state of Idaho, U.S.A.

It did not seem in any way unnatural that Armod should come over and answer explicitly the obvious questions that this collection of anomalies brought to mind. In fact, it took half an hour or more of conversation before Tommy began to realize that his host was consistently replying to his thoughts rather than to his words. It took even longer for him to agree to the simple experiment that started him on his course of study.

But not much longer. An hour after he first entered the hut, Tommy Bender sat staring at eight slips of white paper on which were written, one word to each, the names of eight different objects in the room. The handwriting was careful, precise and clear. Not so the thoughts in Tommy's mind. He had "guessed," accurately, five of the eight objects, holding the faded piece of paper in his hand. He tried to tell himself it was coincidence; that some form of trickery might be involved. *The hand is quicker than the eye.* . . . But it was his own hand that held the paper; he himself unfolded it after making his guess. And Armod's calm certainty was no help in the direction of skepticism.

"Well," Tommy asked uncertainly, "what made you think I could do it?"

"Anyone can do it," Armod said quietly. "For some it is easier than for others. To bring it under control, to learn to do it accurately, every time, is another matter altogether. But the sense is there, in all of us."

Tommy was a bit crestfallen; whether he *believed in it* or not, he preferred to think there was something a bit special about it.

Armod smiled, and answered his disappointment. "For you, it is easier I think than for many others. You are— ah, I despise your psychiatric jargon, but there is no other way to say it so you will understand—you are at ease with yourself. Relaxed. You have few basic conflicts in your personality, so you can reach more easily into the —no it is not the 'subconscious.' It is a part of your mind you have simply not used before. You can use it. You can train it. You need only the awareness of it, and— practice."

Tommy thought that over, slowly, and one by one the implications of it dawned on him.

"You mean I can be a mind reader? Like the acts they do on the stage? I could do it professionally?"

"If you wished to. Few of those who pretend to read minds for the entertainment of others can really do so. Few who have the ability and training would use it in that way. You—ah, you are beginning to grasp some of the possibilities," the old man said, smiling.

"Go on," Tommy grinned. "Tell me what I'm thinking now."

"It would be most . . . indelicate. And . . . I *will* tell you; I do not believe you will have much chance of success, with her. She is an unusual young woman. Others . . . you will be startled, I think, to find how often a forbidding young lady is more hopeful even than willing."

"You're on," Tommy told him. "When do the lessons start, and how much?"

The price was easy; the practice was harder. Tommy gave up smoking entirely, suffered a bit, got over it, and turned his full attention to the procedures involved in gaining "awareness." He lay for hours on his cot, or sat by himself on a lonely hillside in the afternoon sun, learning to sense the presence of every part of himself as fully as that of the world around him.

He learned a dozen different ways of breathing, and discovered how each of them changed, to some slight degree, the way the rest of his body "felt" about things. He found out how to be completely receptive to impressions and sensations from outside himself; and after that, how to exclude them and be aware only of his own functioning organism. He discovered he could *feel* his heart beating and his food digesting, and later imagined he could feel the wound in his leg healing, and thought he was actually helping it along.

This last piece of news he took excitedly to Armod—along with his full ration of cigarettes—and was disappointed to have his mentor receive his excited outpourings with indifference.

"If you waste your substance on such side issues," Armod finally answered his insistence with downright disapproval, "you will be much longer in coming to the true understanding."

Tommy thought that over, swinging back along the jungle path on his crutches, and came to the conclusion that he could do without telepathy a little longer, if he could just walk on his own two feet again. Not that he really believed the progress was anything but illusory—until he heard the medics' exclamations of surprise the next time they changed the cast.

After that, he was convinced. The whole rigamorole was producing some kind of result; maybe it would even, incredibly, do what Armod said it would.

Two weeks later, Tommy got his first flash of certainty. He was, by then, readily proficient in picking thoughts out of Armod's mind; but he knew, too, that the old man was "helping" him . . . maintaining no barriers at all against invasion. Other people had habitual defenses that they didn't even know how to let down. Getting through the walls of verbalization, habitual reaction, hurt, fear and anger, to find out what was really happening inside the mind of a telepathically "inert" person took skill and determination.

That first flash could not in any way be described as "mind reading." Tommy did not hear or read or see any words or images. All he got was a wave of feeling; he was sure it was not his own feeling only because he was just then on his way back from a solitary hillside session in which he had, with considerable thoroughness, identified all the sensations his body then contained.

He was crossing what was laughably referred to as the "lawn"—an area of barren ground decorated with unrootable clumps of tropical weeds, extending from the mess hall to the surgery shack and surrounded by the barracks buildings—when the overwhelming wave of emotion hit him.

It contained elements of affection, interest, and—he checked again to be certain—desire. Desire for a man. He was quite sure now that the feeling was not his, but somebody else's.

He looked about, with sudden dismay, aware for the first time of a difficulty he had not anticipated. That he was "receiving" someone else's emotions he was certain; whose, he did not know.

In front of the surgery shack, a group of nurses stood together, talking. No one else was in sight. Tommy realized, unhappily, that the lady who was currently feeling amorous did not necessarily have to be in his line of vision. He had learned enough about the nature of telepathy by then to understand that it could penetrate physical barriers with relative ease. But he had a hunch. . . .

He had learned enough, too, to understand some part of the meaning of that word, "hunch." He deliberately stopped *thinking*, insofar as he could, and followed his hunch across the lawn to the group of nurses. As he approached them, he let instinct take over entirely. Instead of speaking to them, he made as if to walk by, into the shack.

"Hey there, Lieutenant," one of them called out, and Tommy strained his muscles not to smile with delight. He turned around, innocently, inquiring.

"Surgery's closed now," the little red-headed one said sharply. That wasn't the one who'd called to him. It was the big blonde; he was *almost* sure.

"Oh?" he said. "I was out back of the base, on the hill there, and some damn bug bit me. Thought I ought to get some junk put on it. You never know what's hit you with the kind of skeeters they grow out here." He addressed the remark to the group in general, and threw in a grin that he had been told made him look most appealing like a little boy, meanwhile pulling up the trouser on his good leg to show a fortuitously placed two-day-old swelling. "One leg out of commission is enough for me," he added. "Thought maybe I ought to kind of keep a special eye on the one that still works." He looked up, and smiled straight at the big blonde.

She regarded the area of exposed skin with apparent lack of interest, hesitated, jangled a key in her pocket, and said abruptly, "All right, big boy."

Inside the shack, she locked the door behind them, without appearing to do anything the least bit unusual. Then she got a tube of something out of a cabinet on the wall, and told him to put his leg up on the table.

Right then, Tommy began to understand the real value of what he'd learned, and how to use it. There was nothing in her words or her brisk movements to show him how she felt. While she was smoothing the gooey disinfectant paste on his bite, and covering it with a bandage, she kept up a stream of light talk and banter that gave no clue at all to the way she was appraising him covertly. Tommy had nothing to do but make the proper responses—two sets of them.

Out loud, he described with appropriate humor the monstrous size and appearance of the bug that they both knew hadn't bitten him. But all the time he kept talking and kidding just as if he was still a nice American boy, he could feel her *wanting* him, until he began to get confused between what she wanted and what he did; and his eyes kept meeting hers, unrelated to the words either of them were saying, to let her know he knew.

Each time her hand touched his leg, it was a little more difficult to banter. When it got too difficult, he didn't.

Later, stretched out on his cot in the barracks, he reviewed the entire incident with approval, and made a mental note of one important item. The only overt act the girl made—locking the door—had been accompanied by a strong isolated thought surge of "Don't touch me!" Conversely, the more eager she felt, the more professional she acted. Without the aid of his special one-way window into her mind, he knew he would have made his play at precisely the wrong moment—assuming he'd had the courage to make it at all. As it was, he'd waited till there was no longer any reason for her to believe that he'd even noticed the locking of the door.

That was Lessen Number One about women: *Wait!* Wait till you're sure she's sure. Tommy repeated it happily to himself as he fell asleep that night; and only one small regret marred his contentment. It wasn't Candace. . . .

Lesson Number Two came more slowly, but Tommy was an apt pupil, and he learned it equally well: *Don't wait too long!* The same simple forthright maneuver, he found, that would sweep a normally co-operative young lady literally off her feet if the timing was right would, ten minutes later, earn him nothing more than an indignant slap in the face. By that time, the girl had already decided either that he wasn't interested (insulted); or

that he wasn't experienced enough to do anything about
it (contemptuous); or that he was entirely lacking in
sensitivity, and couldn't possibly understand her at all
(both).

These two lessons Tommy studied assiduously. Between
them, they defined the limits of that most remarkable
point in time, *the Precise Moment*. And the greatest
practical value of his new skill, so far as Tommy could
see, was in being able to locate that point with increasing
accuracy. The most noticeable property of the human
mind is its constant activity; it is a rare man—and notor-
iously an even rarer woman—who has only one point of
view on a given subject, and can stick to it. Tommy discovered soon enough that whatever he was after, whether
it was five bucks to get into a poker game, or a date with
one of the nurses, the best way to get it was to wait for
that particular moment when the other person really
wanted to give it to him.

It should be noted that Tommy Bender retained some
ethics during this period. After the first two games, he
stopped playing poker. Possibly, he was affected by the
fact that suspicious rumors about his "luck" were circulat-
ing too freely; but it is more likely that the game had
lost its punch. He didn't really need the money out there
anyhow. And the process of his embitterment was really
just beginning.

Three weeks after the incident in the surgery shack,
Tommy got his orders for transfer to a stateside hospital.
During that short time, though still impeded by cast and
crutches, he acquired a quantity and quality of experience
with women that more than equaled the total of his
previous successes. And along with it, he suffered a few
shocks.

That Tommy had both manners and ethics has already
been established. He also had morals. He thought he
ought to go to church more often than he did; he took
it for granted that all unmarried women were virgins till
proved otherwise; he never (or hardly ever) used foul
language in mixed company. That kind of thing.

It was, actually, one of the smaller shocks, discovering

the kind of language some of those girls knew. Most of them were nurses, after all, he reminded himself; they heard a lot of guys talking when they were delirious or in pain, but—but that didn't explain how clearly they seemed to understand the words. Or that the ones who talked the most refined were almost always the worst offenders in their minds.

The men's faults he could take in stride; it was the women who dismayed him. Not that he didn't find some "pure" girls; he did, to his horror. But the kind of feminine innocence he'd grown up believing in just didn't seem to exist. The few remaining virgins fell into two categories: those who were so convinced of their own unattractiveness that they didn't even know it when a pass was being made at them; and those who were completely preoccupied with a sick kind of fear-and-loathing that Tommy couldn't even stand to peep at for very long.

Generally speaking, the girls who weren't actually looking for men (which they did with a gratifying but immoral enthusiasm), were either filled with terror and disgust, or were calculating wenches who made their choice for or against the primrose path entirely in terms of the possible profit involved, be it in fast cash or future wedded bliss.

Tommy did find one exception to this generally unpleasant picture. To his determined dismay, and secret pleasure, he discovered that Candace really lived up to his ideal of the American girl. Her mind was a lovely, orderly place, full of softness and a sort of generalized liking for almost everybody. Her thoughts on the subject of most interest to him were also in order: She was apparently well-informed in an impersonal sort of way; ignorant of any personal experience and rather hazily, pleasurably, anticipating the acquisition of that experience in some dim future when she pictured herself as happily in love and married.

As soon as he was quite sure of this state of affairs, Tommy proposed. Candace as promptly declined, and that, for the time being, terminated their relationship. The nurse went about her duties, and whatever personal matters occupied her in her free time. The soldier returned to his pursuit of parapsychology, women and disillusion.

Tommy had no intention of taking these troubles to his teacher. But neither did Armod have to wait for the young man to speak before he knew. This time he was neither stern nor impatient. He spoke once again of the necessity for continuing study till one arrived at the "true understanding," but now he was alternately pleading and encouraging. At one point he was even apologetic.

"I did not know that you would learn so quickly," he said. "If I had foreseen this—doubtless I would have done precisely what I did. One cannot withhold knowledge, and . . ."

He paused, smiling gently and with great sadness. "And the truth of the matter is, you did not ask for knowledge. I offered it. I sold it! Because I could not deny myself the petty pleasure of your cigarettes!"

"Well," Tommy put in uncomfortably, "You made good on it, didn't you? Seems to me you did what you said you would."

"Yes—no," he corrected himself. "I did nothing but show the way. What has been done you did for yourself, as all men must. I cannot see or smell or taste for you; no more could I open the way into men's hearts for you. I gave you a key, let us say, and with it you unlocked the door. Now you look on the other side, but you do not, you can not, understand what you see. It is as though one were to show an infant, just learning to use his eyes, a vision of violent death and bloody birth. He sees, but he does not know. . . ."

Tommy stirred on the low couch, where he could now sit, as the old man did, cross-legged and at ease. But he was uneasy now. He picked up the cane that had replaced the crutches, toying with it, thinking hopefully of departure. Armod understood, and said quickly, "Listen now: I am an old man, and weak in my way. But I have shown you that I have knowledge of a sort. There is much you have yet to learn. If you are to perceive so clearly the depths of the human soul, then it is essential that you learn also to *understand*. . . ."

The old man spoke on; the young one barely listened. He knew he was going home in another week. There was no sense talking about continuing his studies with Armod. And there was no need to continue; certainly no wish to. What he had already learned, Tommy felt, was very likely more than enough. He sat as quietly as he could, being patient till the old man was done talking. Then he stood up, and muttered something about getting back in time for lunch.

Armod shook his head and smiled, still sadly. "You will not hear me. Perhaps you are right. How can I speak to you of the true understanding, when I am still the willing victim of my own body's cravings? I am not fit. I am not fit. . . ."

Tommy Bender was a very disturbed young man. He was getting what he'd wanted, and he didn't like it. He was grateful to Armod, and also angry at him. His whole life seemed to be a string of contradictions.

He drifted along in this unsettled state for the remaining week of his foreign service. Then, in a sudden flurry of affection and making amends, the day he got his orders, he decided to see the old man just once more. Most of the morning he spent racing around the base rounding up all the cigarettes he could get with what cash he had on hand, plus a liberal use of the new skills Armod had taught him. Then he got his gear together quickly. He was due at the air strip at 1400 hours, and at 1130 he left the base for a last walk to the village, the cane in one hand, two full cartons of butts in the other.

He found Armod waiting for him in a state of some agitation, apparently expecting him. There ensued a brief formal presentation of Tommy's gift, and acceptance of it; then for the last time, the old man invited him to drink tea, and ceremoniously set the water to simmer in the copper pot.

They both made an effort, and managed to get through the tea-drinking with no more than light polite talk. But when Tommy stood up to leave, Armod broke down.

"Come back," he begged. "When you are free of your service, and have funds to travel, come back to study again."

"Why, sure, Armod," Tommy said. "Just as soon as I can manage it."

"Yes, I see. This is what they call a social lie. It is meant not to convince me, but to terminate the discussion. But listen, I beg you, one moment more. You can see and hear in the mind now; but you cannot talk, nor can you keep silence. Your own mind is open to all who come and know how to look—"

"Armod, please, I—"

"You can learn to project thought as I do. To build a barrier against intrusion. You can—"

"Listen, Armod," Tommy broke in determinedly again. "I don't have to know any of that stuff. In my home town, there isn't anybody else who can do this stuff. And there's no reason for me to ever come back here. Look, I'll tell you what I can do. When I get back home, I can send you all the cigarettes you want—"

"No!"

The old man jumped up from his mat on the floor, and took two rapid strides to the shelf where Tommy's present lay. He picked up the two cartons, and tossed them contemptuously across the room, to land on the couch next to the soldier.

"No!" he said again, just a little less shrilly. "I do not want your cigarettes! I want nothing, do you understand? Nothing for myself! Only to regain the peace of mind I have lost through my weakness! Go to another teacher, then," he was struggling for calm. "There are many others. In India. In China. Perhaps even in your own country. Go to one who is better fitted than I. But do not stop now! You can learn more, much more!"

He was trembling with emotion as he spoke, his skinny frame shaking, his black eyes popping as though they would burst out of his head. "As for your cigarettes," he concluded, "I want none of them. I vow now, until the day I die, I shall never again give way to this weakness!"

He was a silly, excitable old man, who was going to regret these words. Tommy stood up feeling the foolish apologetic grin on his face and unable to erase it. He did not pick up the cigarettes.

"Good-bye Armod," he said, and walked out for the last time through the blue-topped door.

But whatever either of them expected, and regardless of Tommy's own wishes, his education did not stop there. It had already gone too far to stop. The perception-awareness process seemed to be self-perpetuating, and though he practiced his exercises no more, his senses continued to become more acute—both the physical and the psychological.

At the stateside hospital, where his leg rapidly improved, Tommy had some opportunity to get out and investigate the situation with the nice old-fashioned girls who'd stayed at home and didn't go to war. By that time, he could "see" and "hear" pretty clearly.

He didn't like what he found.

That did it, really. All along, out at the base hospital, he'd clung to the notion that the women at home would be different—that girls so far from civilization, were exposed to all sorts of indecencies a nice girl never had to face, and *shouldn't* have to. Small wonder they turned cynical and evil-minded.

The girls at home, he discovered, were less of the first, and far more of the second.

When Tommy Bender got home again, he was grimly determined and firmly disillusioned. He knew what he wanted out of life, saw no hope at all of ever getting it, and had very few scruples about the methods he used to get the next-best things.

In a remarkably short time, he made it clear to his erstwhile friends and neighbors that he was almost certain to get anything he went after. He made money; he made love; and of course he made enemies. All the while, his friends and neighbors tried to understand. Indeed, they thought they did. A lot of things can happen to a man when he's been through hell in combat, and then had to

spend months rotting and recuperating in a lonely Far
Eastern field hospital.

But of course they couldn't even begin to understand
what had happened to Tommy. They didn't know what
it was like to live on a steadily plunging spiral of anger
and disillusionment, all the time liking people less, and
always aware of how little they liked you.

To sign a contract with a man, knowing he would de-
fraud you if he could; he couldn't, of course, because you
got there first. But when you met him afterward, you
_ _ _ _ _ _ the blast of hate and envy he threw at you.

To make love to a woman, and know she was the wrong
woman for you or you the wrong man for her. And then
to meet her afterward . . .

Tommy had in the worst possible sense, got out of
bed on the wrong side. When he first awoke to the
knowledge of other people's minds, _ _ had seen ugliness
and fear wherever he looked, and that first impress of
bitterness on his own mind had colored everything he
had seen since.

For almost five years after he came home, Tommy
Bender continued to build a career, and ruin reputations.
People tried to understand what had happened to him
. . . but how could they?

Then something happened. It started with an envelope
in his morning mail. The envelope was marked "Personal," so it was unopened by his secretary, and left on
the side of his desk along with three or four other thin,
squarish, obviously non-business, envelopes. As a result,
Tommy didn't read it till late that afternoon, when he
was trying to decide which girl to see that night.

The return address said "C. Harper, Hotel Albemarle,
Topeka, Kansas." He didn't know anyone in Topeka, but
the name Harper was vaguely reminiscent. He was in-
trigued enough to open that one first, and the others
never were opened at all.

"Dear Tommy," it read. "First of all, I hope you still
remember me. It's been quite a long time, hasn't it? I just
heard, from Lee Potter (the little, dark girl who came
just before you left . . . remember her?)"—Tommy did,

with some pleasure—"that you were living in Hartsdale, and had some real-estate connections there. Now I'd like to ask a favor. . . .

"I've just had word that I've been accepted as Assistant Superintendent of the Public Health Service there—in Hartsdale—and I'm supposed to start work on the 22nd. The only thing is, I can't leave my job here till just the day before. So I wondered if you could help me find a place to stay beforehand? Sort of mail-order real estate service?

"I feel I'm being a little presumptuous, asking this, when perhaps you don't even remember me—but I do hope you won't mind. And please don't go to any special trouble. From what Lee said, I got the idea this might be right in your line of business. If it's not, don't worry. I'm sure I can find something when I get there.

"And thanks, ahead of time, for anything you can do.

"Cordially," it concluded, "Candace Harper."

Tommy answered the letter the same day, including a varied list of places and prices hurriedly worked up by his real-estate agent. That he owned real estate was true; that he dealt in it, not at all. His letter to Candy did not go into these details. Just told her how vividly he remembered her, and how good it would be to see her again, with some questions about the kind of furnishings and décor she'd prefer. "If you're going to get in early enough on the 21st," he wound up, "how about having dinner with me? Let me know when you're coming, anyhow. I'd like to meet you, and help you get settled."

For the next eleven days, Tommy lived in an almost happy whirl of preparation, memory and anticipation. In all the years since he had proposed to Candace, he had never met another girl who filled so perfectly the mental image of the ideal woman with which he had first left home. He kept telling himself she wouldn't, couldn't, still be the same person. Even a non-telepath would get bitter and disillusioned in five years of the Wonderful Post-War World. She *couldn't* be the same. . . .

And she wasn't. She was older, more understanding,

more tolerant, and if possible warmer and pleasanter than before. Tommy met her at the station, bought her some dinner, took her to the perfect small apartment where she was, unknown to herself, paying only half the rent. He stayed an hour, went down to run some errands for her, stayed another half-hour, and knew by then that in the most important respects she hadn't changed at all.

There wasn't going to be any "Precise Moment" with Candy; not that side of a wedding ceremony.

Tommy couldn't have been more pleased. Still, he was cautious. He didn't propose again till three weeks later, when he'd missed seeing her two days in a row due to business-social affairs. If they were married, he could have taken her along.

When he did propose, she lived up to all his qualifications again. She said she wanted to think it over. What she thought was: Oh, yes! Oh, yes, he's the one I want! But it's too quick! How do I know for sure? He never even thought of me all this time . . . all the time I was waiting and hoping to hear from him . . . how can he be sure so soon? He might be sorry. . . .

"Let me think about it a few days, will you, Tommy?" she said, and he was afraid to take her in his arms for fear he'd crush her with his hunger.

Four weeks later they were married. And when Candy told him her answer, she also confessed what he already knew: that she'd regretted turning him down ever since he left the field hospital; that she'd been thinking of him, loving him, all the long years in between.

Candy was a perfect wife, just as she had been a perfect nurse, and an all-too-perfect dream girl. The Benders' wedding was talked about for years afterwards; it was one of those rare occasions when everything turned out just right. And the bride was so beautiful. . . .

The honeymoon was the same way. They took six weeks to complete a tour of the Caribbean, by plane, ship and car. They stayed where they liked as long as they liked, and did what they liked, all the time. And not once in those six weeks was there any serious difference in what they liked. Candy's greatest wish at every point

was to please Tommy, and that made things very easy
for both of them.

And all the while, Tommy was gently, ardently, in-
structing his lovely bride in the arts of matrimony. He
was tender, patient and understanding, as he had known
beforehand he would have to be. A girl who gets to the
age of twenty-six with her innocence intact is bound to
require a little time for readjustment.

Still, by the time they came back, Tommy was beginning to feel a sense of failure. He knew that Candace had
yet to experience the fulfillment she had hoped for, and
that he had planned to give her.

Watching her across the breakfast table on the dining
terrace of their new home, he was enthralled as ever. She
was lovely in negligee, her soft hair falling around her
face, her eyes shining with true love as they met his.

It was a warm day, and he saw, as he watched her, the
tiny beads of sweat form on her upper lip. It took him
back . . . way back . . . and from the vividness of the hospital scene, he skipped to an equally clear memory of
that last visit to Armod, the teacher.

He smiled, and reached for his wife's hand, wondering
if ever he would be able to tell her what had come of
that walk they took to the village together. And he
pressed her hand tighter, smiling again, as he realized
that now, for the first time, he had a use for the further
talents the old man had promised him.

That would be one way to show Candace the true
pleasure she did not yet know. If he could project his
own thoughts and emotions . . .

He let go of her hand, and sat back, sipping his coffee,
happy and content, with just the one small problem to
think about. *Maybe I should have gone back for a while,
after all,* he thought idly.

"Perhaps you should have, dear," said innocent Candace. "I did."

THE LADY
WAS A
TRAMP

SHE HAD
been lovely once, sleek-lined and proud, with shining
flanks; and men had come to her with hungry hearts and
star-filled eyes, and high pulse of adventure in their blood.

Now she was old. Her hide was scarred with use, her
luster dulled; though there was beauty in her still it was
hidden deep. A man had to know where to look—and he
had to care.

The young man left the conditioned coolness of the
Administration Building and paused outside the door to
orient. Then he strode briskly forward, ignoring the heat
that wilted his uniform collar and damply curled the
edges of the freshly stamped papers in his breast pocket.
He passed the inner tier of docks, refusing to look to
left or right at the twin proud heights of gleaming Navy
vessels.

Beyond them, alone in the outmost ring, the *Lady Jane*
sat on her base in the concrete hole, waiting. In the
white-light glare of the shadowless Dome, each smallest
pit and pockmark of twenty years' usage stood out in
cruel relief against the weathered darkness of her hull.
Potbellied, dumpy, unbeautiful, she squatted without
impatience inside the steel framework of supports, while
her tanks were flushed and her tubes reamed clean. When
the dock gang was done, and the ravages of the last
voyage repaired insofar as could be, she would set forth
once more on her rounds of the ports in space. Meantime, she rested.

47

The young man paused. It was his first good look at the Lady Jane. He half-turned back; but it was too late now. Fury, or training, or despair, or some of all of them, moved him on.

"That's him all right," Anita smiled, and turned a knob on the *Lady Jane's* viewpoint screen; the figure leaped toward them with focussed clarity, and the IBMan insignia showed up on the jacket sleeve.

"Mad dogs and eye-bee-men," Chan quoted softly, and leaned forward to study the young man with mock amazement. On the tenth "day" of Lunar sunlight it was still possible to keep moderately cool inside an unsealed ship, and the central Administration Building was kept at a steady seventy, day or night. But out in the atmosphere dome, it was *hot*. Yet the young man walking briskly toward the ship wore formal greens, and his shirt was bound at his neck with a knotted tie. Chandra leaned back, picked up a tall cold glass and shook his head.

"Look at him, Chan! He's a *kid*. . . ."

Chan shrugged. "You knew that before. You got the papers. . . ."

Impatiently, she shook her head. "I know. But *look* at him. . . ."

"I wasn't any older." Chandra began.

"Yes you were! I don't know what your papers said, but—look at him. A⸺ weren't an IBMan. And we were all younger then. And—darling, you were a *man!*"

He laughed and stood up, rumpling her hair as he passed. "Well, if that's all that's eating on you, babe—hell, four of us kept you happy half-way home."

He ducked through the bunk-room door as she started to rise. "Don't shoot," he called back.

"It ain't so funny, honey." She stood watching the screen. "What's bothering me is, who's going to keep *him* happy?"

Terence Hugh Carnahan, Lieutenant, U.N.N. Reserves, was twenty-four years old and newly commissioned. He was stuffed to the gills with eight full years of Academy training, precision, and knowledge. The shiny new stripes on his sleeve and the dampening papers inside his breast pocket were the prizes he'd worked for and dreamed of as long as it mattered. The fruits were sour now, and the dream was curdled. A man might approach the Lady incited by lust to a venture of greed; but the sight of her was enough to wipe out the last visions of glory.

The Lieutenant moved on, more slowly. He stopped as a three-wheeled red-and-white-striped baggage truck swung out in a wide crazy curve from behind the Navy ship to the left and careened to a stop at the Lady's side.

A tall thin man in rumpled full-dress whites leaped out of the bucket, swinging a canvas suitcase in his hand. He climbed aboard the ship's waiting elevator and it started up.

Terry walked on and waited beside the truck for the cage to come down. When it did, he produced his ID card, got inside, and rode up in silence.

In the open lock, the man in the dirty whites was waiting for him. He held out his hand, and for the first time Terry saw the pilot's jets on his lapels; and the boards on his shoulders spelled Commander.

"You the new IBMan?" the pilot asked. "... gear?"

"I sent it on this morning." They shook, and the pilot's slim fingers were unexpectedly cool and dry.

"Welcome to our happy home," he said. "Glad to have you aboard. And all that sort of thing. Manuel Ramon Decardez, at your service. They call me Deke."

"I'm Terry Carnahan."

"Come on in. I guess they're all waiting." Deke led the way through the open inner valve.

In the suit room, the pilot turned back. "Just take it easy, kid," he said. "It ain't like the Navy in here."

It wasn't.

The Lieutenant had been on merchant ships before. It was part of his training to know the layout and standard equipment of every jump-ship ever made. He had been on inspection tours; and a Lady class ship was still in

Academy use for cadet instruction trips. But that one was Navy-maintained and Navy-staffed.

This *Lady* had left the service thirteen years back. The crew quarters had been torn out to make an extra hold, and the rule book had gone by the wayside along with the hammocks.

"Up here," Deke said, and Terry followed him up the ladder to Officers' Country. Then he stood in the wardroom doorway and stared at the crazy carnival scene.

To start with, the overheads were off. The only light was diffused U-V out of the algy tanks that cut two-foot swaths along opposite bulkheads. In the yellow-green dimness, the scattered lounging chairs and coffee cups and a tray with a bottle and glasses on the table, gave a ridiculous cocktail-bar effect to the whole place. And the first thing he saw was a hippy blonde, in tight black slacks and a loosely tied white shirt, who detached herself from the arm of a chair—and from the encircling arm of what looked like a naked brown-skinned man inside the chair. She ran across the room to fling herself on Deke, who picked her up bodily, kissed her with gusto.

"Where did you sneak in from?" she demanded. "We were waiting for—"

"Whoa, babe," Deke started. "If you mean—" He started to turn, began to move forward, to let Terry in, but from a shadowy corner a wiry little man in coveralls, with grease-stains on his hands and his hair and his face, broke in.

"What the hell! These two give me a pile of pitch about haulin' myself up here to give the new kid a big hello, and all I find is *this* old s.o.b. instead!" These two appeared to be the blonde and the naked man. Deke was the s.o.b.

"You bitchin' again, Mike?" The voice was a bull-roar; it came from the only member of the *Lady's* crew Terry had met before. The Captain came down the ladder from Control, sneakers and rolled-cuff workpants first, and then the tremendous bulk of chest and arms, bristled with wiry curling red-gold hair. The room had looked crowded before. With Karl Hillstrom's two-hundred-twenty pounds added, it was jammed. "Relax," he said. "Have a drink and relax. Nita said she saw the kid comin' . . ."

Deke had given up trying to interrupt. He turned back to Terry and shrugged. "I told you—" he started, and just then the blonde saw him.

"Oh, my God!" she said, and broke into helpless laughter; so did Deke. She took a step forward toward Terry, trying to talk. He ignored it.

"Captain Hillstrom?" he said formally, as loud as possible. He felt like a school-kid in a lousy play, doing a bad job of acting the part of the butler at a masquerade.

The big man turned. "Oh, there you are!" He held out a burly hand. "You met Deke already? Anita, this is our new IBMan, Terry Carnahan. Anita Filmord, our Medic. And Mike Gorevitch, our Chief—" that — the grease-stained one—"and Chan—Chandra Lal, our Biotech."

Terry fished in his pocket for the orders the Captain had failed to request, and noted with relief meantime that the Biotech, Chan, now unfolding himself from his chair, wasn't entirely naked after all.

It wasn't till then that he fully realized the hippy blonde was nobody's visiting daughter or friend, but a member of the crew and an officer in the Naval Reserve.

The blonde officer put a drink in his hand, and his last clear thought that night was that Deke was quite right: it wasn't like the Navy. Not at all.

When they gave him his commission, at the Examiner's Board, they had also delivered elaborate and resounding exhortations about the Great Trust being placed this day in his hands: how the work of an IBMan on a merchant ship was both more difficult and more important by far than anything done by an officer of equivalent rank on a Navy ship.

He knew all that. The ranking IBMan officer, on any ship, was fully responsible for the operation and maintenance of all material connected in any way with either solar navigation or space-warp jumps. On a tramp, there was likely to be just one IBMan to do it all, Navy Transports carried a full complement of four officers and five enlisted men. Fresh Academy graduates came on board with j.g. status only, and worked in charge of an enlisted maintenance crew on the "jump-along"—that abstract mechanical brain whose function it was to set up the obscure mathematic-symbolic relationships which made it possible for matter to be transmitted through the "holes" in space-time, enabling a ship to travel an infinite distance in an infinitesimal time.

On a Navy transport, a full Lieutenant IBMan would be in charge of SolNav only, with two petty officers under him, both qualified to handle maintenance, and one at least with a Navy rating, capable of relieving him on duty at the control board during the five or twelve or twenty hours it might take to navigate a jump-ship in or out of the obstacle course of clutter and junk and planets and orbits of any given System.

Even the senior officer, on a Navy Transport, would never have to jump "blind," except in the rare and nearly unheard-of instance of an analog failure; only tramps and Navy Scouts ever jumped willingly on anything but a 'log-computed course. The stellar analog computers were the Navy's Topmost Secret; when you used one, nothing was required except to make sure the jump-along itself was in perfect condition, and then to pull the switch. The 'log did the rest.

Merchant ships carried 'logs for their chartered ports of call—the *Lady* had two—but the charter ports were the smallest part of a merchant trip. The number of destinations for which Navy analogs were available was hardly a hatfull out of the galaxies. Without a 'log to point the way for him, it was up to the IBMan to plot coordinates for where a hole *ought* to be. With luck and skill he could bring the ship out into normal space again somewhere within SolNav reach of the destination. With the tiniest error in computation, a ship might be lost forever in some distant universe with no stars to steer her home.

Terry Carnahan had been hoping desperately for a Navy transport job—but only because it was the route to the Scouts: the Navy's glory-boys, the two-bunk blind-jump ships that went out alone to map the edges of man's universe. It was the Scout job he'd worked for those long eight years—and dreamed about five years before, while he sweated for credits to get into Academy.

He didn't argue with his tramp assignment; nobody argued with the Board. He knew that most of the men who drew Navy assignments would envy him; the money was in the Reserves. And most of the rest, the ones who drew Transport and liked it, were there because they couldn't jump blind, and they knew it.

He knew all that. But when his orders came, and they told him he drew a tramp because he was tenth in his class—that's what they said: tramp work was the toughest —he also knew how close he had come to the dream, because he also knew that the top five men had been sent to Scout training.

Eight years of the most he could give it just wasn't enough. The answer was NO! For good.

But you didn't throw out eight years of training for a good job either. Terry went for his psychs and medics, and met Captain (U.N.N. Reserve) Karl Hillstrom; he took his two weeks' leave and reported for duty.

That first night, he fell asleep with the bunkroom spinning around him, and an obvious simple solution to the whole mess spinning with it, just out of his reach, no matter how fast he turned. When he stopped whirling, the dreams began, the dreams about naked crewmen, one of whom might have been him, and a terrible wonderful blonde in a sea of stars, winkin' and blinkin' and nod in a herring tramp to the smiling moon-faced girl who asked him in. . . .

In the morning, Captain Karl Hillstrom showed him around Control. It was ship-shape and shiny up here, and the IBMan plunged gratefully into routine, checking and testing his board, and running off sample comps. He allowed himself only the briefest inspection of the jump-along and the keyboard and calckers attached. His first job would be solar navigation. Once they were clear of the System, there'd be three weeks on solar drive before they jumped—plenty of time to double-check the other equipment. Right now, the standard computers and solar 'log were what counted.

He worked steadily till he became aware of the Captain at his side.

"How does it look?"

"Fine so far, sir." Terry leaned back.

"Anything messed up there, you can blame it on me. I worked that board coming in."

Terry remembered now—they had lost their IBMan on Betelgeuse IV, last trip, and come back short-handed, and with half the trade load still in the holds. Since no one but an IBMan could jump blind, they'd had to come back to pick up a new man—Terry.

"I haven't found anything wrong, sir," Terry said.

"You can drop the 'sir.' We go mostly by first names here." There was an edge of irritation in the Captain's voice. "It's chow time now. You want to knock off?"

Terry hesitated. This wasn't the Navy; it was a lousy tramp. If the pilot was drunk half the time, and the Chief had a dirty neck, and the Captain looked like a pirate or stevedore (the first of which he was, and the second had been), the IBMan was certainly free to work or eat when he chose.

"I'd just as lief stick with it for a while," Terry said cautiously.

"Sure. Suit yourself. Galley's open. Take what you want when you want it. . . ."

He disappeared. For a blessed two hours, alone with machines he knew and trusted, Terry ran off the standard tests and comps, noting with trained percision each tiniest deviation from perfect performance. The computer had never been built that could navigate without error. Maybe only in the tenth decimal, but that was enough for disaster. You had to know your 'log and your board and machines, and make your adjustments as automatically as a man makes allowance for the sights on a rifle he's known and shot for years.

It took Terry four hours to learn this board, and he had started his first dry-run when the sandwich appeared on his arm-rest. A tall plastic glass with a straw in the top and a tempting froth came next.

"Well, thanks," he said, "but you didn't have to—"

"It's chocolate," she told him. "I ordered strawberry when your papers came in, but they haven't sent it yet."

"Chocolate is fine," he said weakly, and let himself look.

The loose-tied shirt and tight-fitting slacks of the evening had been replaced by standard-issue summer-weight fatigues. The blouse was zipped up, and she seemed to be wearing a bra underneath. Her shorts displayed no more than a reasonable length of shapely leg. She wore no makeup, and her face looked scrubbed and clean. You could hardly get mad at a woman for being good-looking. The sandwich looked toasted and crisp, and he found he was very hungry.

"Well, thanks," he said again, and took a bite, and picked up the pencil with his other hand.

"Karl had to go down to Ad," she said. He took his eyes off his paper, and figured that out. Administration office, she'd mean.

"They called him to bring down the Beetle 'log papers," she said. "He asked me to let you know—it'll be back in the morning."

He nodded, trying to match her casual air. The Betel-geuse analog was coming back from the shop tomorrow. And IBMan Carnahan would be due for his first installation—the first on his own command.

". . . we could finish your med-check in time for dinner," she was talking still. "You want to knock off up here pretty soon?"

He nodded again, and glanced over his board. The run he'd started would take most of an hour. Then some time for adjustments. . . . "Sixteen hours all right?" he asked.

"Fine. Dinner's at nineteen."

He sat there and stared at his sandwich and thought it all over, including the staggering fact of the Commander's silver leaves on the woman's faded green shirt collar.

The milkshake turned out to be good; the sandwich delicious. The run on the board got fouled up, and after a half an hour of grief, he had to admit his mind wasn't on it. There was a Manual on the wardroom shelf below, that would tell him the things he wanted to know. He switched off the board, and went down.

Page 532, Section six, was explicit. The Medical Officer for a six-man crew had to have junior psych, as well as a senior pharmacist's or nurse's rating—*besides* being qualified sub for the Biotech. With Commander's rank, it meant she likely had more actual years of training than he did. And: "The Medical Officer shall be supplied with dossiers . . . psych ratings and personality profiles . . . responsible for well-being of personnel. . . ."

It explained some things: the milk shake and strawberry order, for instance; and why she should bother with either one. It did nothing to change the first impression of last night; or to make him forget his dreams; or —certainly—to make him feel any more at ease with Commander Anita Filmord. There were some things a woman shouldn't know about a man . . . or at least *some* women. . . .

There was very little Anita Filmord didn't know about Terry Carnahan three hours later. For the first half-hour she took smears and samples and scrapings with deft impersonal proficiency. Each labeled slide or tube went into its own slot or niche or clamp; then she threw a switch, and sat down to confront him with a questionnaire. To the familiar humming background of the diagnostics, she asked him all the questions he had answered twice a year for the past eight years.

"They put me through all this when I got my orders," he said at the end. "How come . . ."

"We do it every time you come on board. I'll have to run samples on Karl this evening too." The machine had run itself down. She pulled out the tape, tossed it onto her desk for reading later. "*I* don't know what you've been doing the past two weeks," she pointed out, and he felt himself flush at the certainty of what she meant. "And we've got a good long time to be shut up on this ship together." She stood there looking at him. Her smile faded. "The prospect isn't too appealing, is it?"

"You are!" he might have said. This wasn't the Navy. The way she was dressed last night, the way she acted . . .

Last night—was it one of those dreams? He couldn't be sure, but the memory came clearly. . . . He had heard a door close, and the murmur of voices, one high and one low. Before he fell asleep again—or in his dream?—a tall figure had entered the bunkroom and flopped in the last empty sack.

Five men and one woman . . .

"*You're goddam right it's not!*" he wanted to say, but he shifted his gaze four inches, and the leaves on the collar of her short-sleeved shirt were still a Commander's.

He threw out all putative answers, and retreated to subordination.

"Yes, ma'am," he said blank-faced. "It surely is, ma'am." *Five men and one woman . . . and Deke had it all tied up! . . .*

"I'm glad to hear you say so, Lieutenant," she answered deadpan. "But if anything *should* turn up—any problems or questions or troubles of any kind—remember, that's why I'm here." Her smile was just a bit mechanical this time. *Good!*

"Just come if you need me," she said. "Any time . . ."

Five men and one woman . . . and come, she said, any time . . . maybe it wasn't just Deke. Maybe . . .

He went to the spray room and stripped and turned on the shower full blast to shut out Chandra Lal's cheerful talk. When he was finished, Chan was still in a cloud of steam, the effects of a day cleaning algy tanks now removed. While Terry rubbed himself harshly dry, Chan resumed conversation.

"How do you like the old bitch?" he asked idly.

"I'm not an expert," Carnahan said, and rubbed faster.

"Who is? I've been here six years now, and I still get surprises. She may not look like much, but she's a hell of a mess of boat for five men to run. . . .

Five men and one woman . . . What the hell? Come

off that track, boy. Chan was talking about the ship—not the Medic.

"You're right about that," Terry said, and escaped to his locker.

He wore his clean uniform like armor into the wardroom, accepted a cocktail, and sipped at it slowly. Deke, the pilot, and Captain Hillstrom were both drunk already, loudly replaying the ball game they'd just seen on the vid.

Hillstrom had shed his uniform as soon as he got back in the ship; he was bare-chested and rolled-cuffed again.

Deke at least dressed for dinner. So did Anita. Tonight, the tight-ass slacks were red, and she did wear a bra—also bright red—under her clear plastic shirt.

Mike wasn't dressed and he wasn't drunk. He came up just in time to sit down and eat with the rest, his face and coveralls both, if possible, one layer greasier than the day before. Chandra did not dress either: he emerged from the spray room, glowing, immaculate in the virtually non-existent trunks he'd worn the night before. Anita poured him a drink.

Obviously, she wouldn't care how—or if—Chan was dressed.

And if she didn't, who should?

Not Karl Hillstrom, that was clear; or perhaps he was too drunk to notice. . . .

Sleep didn't come easy that night. When all the crew's bunks but Deke's were filled, Terry gave up, and went out to the wardroom. He found Deke there, alone, watching a film. He tried to watch, too, but next to the screen, a red light on the Medic's door flashed, DON'T DISTURB! and his eyes kept seeing, instead of the picture, the curve of a thigh limned in the fiery red of her slacks, or perhaps of the bulb. . . .

He got up and prowled the room.

DON'T DISTURB: ". . . any time . . ."

The door opened. Karl Hillstrom came out. It closed behind him, and the light flicked off. She was alone now. She could be disturbed.

"Hi . . . late-late show?" Karl poured himself a drink and held up the bottle. "How about you?"

"I had it," Deke said.

"Terry?"

"Thanks. I will . . . later." He poured his own, a big one, and took it back to his bunk.

. . . any time . . . Deke didn't have it tied up, not at all. . . .

At two in the morning, he remembered vaguely some provision in the Manual for refusal to serve in ships with a crew of less than ten, on grounds of personality stress. That meant a psych Board of course—and it had to go through the Medic . . . well, she might have reasons to make it easy for him. This wasn't the Navy, but it was still under Navy charter. Lousy tramp! He grinned, and promised himself to look it up, and went to sleep.

At three, he woke briefly, remembering she had said the Captain would have to have a new set of samples run that evening for his med records. Well, that could explain the DON'T DISTURB . . . At eight, they woke him to tell him the Beetle 'log was coming on board.

Mike Gorevitch drifted up from his engines to lend a hand, and the hand was a steady one, Terry found. By noon they were finished with a job that would have taken Terry more than a day by himself. His first installation was finished. Over a shared plate of cold meat in the galley, the IBMan found himself inexplicably pleased the Chief's terse invitation to have a look below.

"Nothin' you didn't see before better on a Navy boat," Mike said, "But some of the stuff is rigged up my own way. You ever get stuck with a duty shift down there, you'll want to know . . ."

Like every jump-ship, the Lady was Navy built, equipped, and staffed. Even Hillstrom, who had made his stake in the Solar Fleet, had to get his Reserve Commission before they'd sell him his ship and lease him a stellar analog to hook onto the jump-along.

By now he had traded in that first cheap Sirius 'log for a prized Aldebaran, and had acquired a Betelgeuse besides. It was on Betelgeuse IV that Bailey, the IBMan who'd been with the Lady for nine of her thirteen years tramping, had lost his nerve. It was something that happened. The best jump-man reached the point where he'd figured he'd had it—the one more blind trip wouldn't work. Bailey quit cold, and declined even passage back.

This trip, the Lady carried a consignment of precision instruments for the new colony on Aldebaran III. But nobody ever got rich on consignment freight. It paid for the trip; that was all. The profit-shares came out of the other hold: the seeds and whisky and iron pigs and glassware and quick-freeze livestock embryos; the anything-and-whatsit barter goods that someone at some unchartered planet off the Analog routes would pay for in some way. That was the lure that kept the crews on merchant ships: you never knew when you'd come back with the barter-hold full of uranium, or cast-gold native artifacts, or robin-egg diamonds.

And if you also never knew for sure when you'd come back, or where from, or whether . . . well, that was the reason why IBMen went upstairs fast. For a man who could handle the job, there was pay and promotion, and almost anything else he might want.

What Carnahan wanted, the Lady didn't have.

For Mike Gorevitch, that was not the case.

The Lady was a tramp. She was scratched and dented and tarnished with age. She'd lost her polish, and her shape was out of date. She'd been around, and it showed.

But she had beauty in her still, if you knew where to look, and you cared.

"There's a dance in the old girl yet," Mike said approvingly, when he saw the IBMan's hand linger with pleasure on the smooth perfect surface of the shaft he'd ground the night before. "You read Archy?" he asked.

Terry shook his head. "What's that?"

"You might not like it," Mike said doubtfully. He opened a locker and pulled out a battered grease-stained book. "Here. You can take it up with you if you want."

That night, Terry slept. He took the Manual and Mike's book both to the bunk with him right after dinner, and found what he wanted in one, then returned to the other. Both of them helped, and so did exhaustion.

But somewhere in the night he woke long enough to note that it was Deke who came in last again, and to identify the pattern of repeated sounds from two nights back. It had not been a dream.

Five men and one woman . . . He wondered why Bailey had quit. Nine years, and then . . . If you took it that long . . . Well, he had the same way out if he wanted it . . . any time . . .

Next day, again, he worked at his board through the morning. This time it was Chandra who happened to be in the galley when Terry went down for his lunch. The pattern began to come clear: informal, haphazard, and unsystematic, but they were taking him over the ship, little by little.

The two of them sat on a white-painted bench in the Bio lab, and discoursed of algae and alien life-forms and also Anita. "Listen," Chan said abruptly, "has the blonde ho-hohell got you mixed up?"

"No," Terry said bitterly. "I wouldn't say that."

"It ain't like the Navy, is it kid?" Chan smiled, and it didn't matter if you knew the man had been trained for years to create just this feeling of empathy and understanding; he created it all the same. If he couldn't, they'd be in a hell of a spot on an alien planet. . . .

"Don't get me wrong," Terry said cautiously. "I like girls. If you think everyone sleeps in his own bed on a Navy ship . . ."

"I came out of Academy too," Chan reminded him.

"All right, then, you know what I mean. But this kind of deal—one dame, and the five of us, and—I just can't see it. If I go to a whore, I don't want her around me all day. And if I have a girl, I damn sure don't want every guy she sees to get into . . . you know what I mean!"

"Yeah." He was silent a moment. "I know what you mean, but I don't know if I can explain . . . Look, it's a small ship, and the payload counts. A girl friend for every guy would be nice, but . . . well, hell, kid, you'll see for yourself once we get going. All I wanted to say to begin with was if you got the idea it was all for one guy, you were wrong. Deke's always kind of hopped up before we go, and he's the guy we have to count on to get us out safe. She just naturally . . . anyhow, don't let him monopolize anything—not if you want it, that is."

"I don't," Terry said, and they went back to algae and aliens. And at least one thing emerged: Mike wasn't the only man on board who cared. Just what it was that mattered so much to him or to Chan, Terry wasn't quite sure: their work, or the Lady herself, or the dead dream she stood for. Whatever exactly it was, the feeling was something that Terry could understand—and that Deke and Hillstrom never could . . .

Hillstrom didn't have to. He owned the Lady. He wasn't obliged to understand her: only to pay the bills, and let the hired hands do their work for him. For her . . . ?

The hired help worked, all right. At least, Mike and Chan did, and Terry Carnahan. Even Deke put in a full morning up in Control, checking his board, and testing a dry run with Terry.

Even Deke? What the hell? Deke had been holding down the driver's seat on the Lady for four years now. He had to be good. And he was; the half-hour's test was enough to show his class.

In his bunk that night, Terry improved his acquaintance with Archy the poet-cockroach, and Mehitabel the cat. Archy's opinions amused him; but in the determined dignity of the lady-cat's earthy enthusiasms, he found a philosophy sadly appropriate for the life of a Lady ship: and it was difficult to continue to feel entirely sad about the fit of the shoe while Mehitabel danced her wild free whirling dance, defiant and tourjoursgai . . . wotthehell . . . wotthehell . . .

Mehitabel, Mike, and Chandra all helped. But backing them all up was the Manual.

P. 549, at the bottom: "An IBMan specialist may exercise his privilege of declaring the psychological conditions on board a ship of the specified classes unfit for blind jump at any time before plotting navigation data

dream of sunshine and sparkling water. Zero *minus nine*, and he sat up erect. *Minus eight*, and he forced himself back into limpness before they hit *seven*. Breathe in . . . out . . . hold . . . in . . . six . . . out . . . hold . . . in . . . hold . . . five . . . out . . . four . . . in . . . *three* . . . out . . . two . . . innnnnone-annnnou—out!

Off and out . . . down and out . . . blackness and whirl-pools and terror and kick back, up, out!

His finger punched the wake-up button before he was fully aware of consciousness again. The light ahead of him flashed green, and there was an instant's prideful notice that his was the second green on. Then he forgot to be proud, and forgot to be Terry Carnahan. Green lights flashed and steadied, then yellow and blue and red. The board was a Christmas-tree crossword constellation, each light a word or a number or place, their shifting patterns spelling out death and life.

Pressure eased; and the voices began—voices of engines and scanners and stresses and temps. Some he heard in the helmet and some the board told him with signals and lights. A voice in the helmet allowed him to take it off: the voice of the Bio board. A key on the pilot's board, at the chair up ahead, was depressed by a finger; the *think*-board, in this chair, flashed questioning lights. The *think*-board replied, and new figures lit up ahead, for the hands to use—the hands and direction and eyes of the Lady, up there at the pilot's board, steering her free of the multi-tude of menacing mites and pieces and bits of matter and mass in the populous planet-plied system.

The dance of escape begat rhythm to suit itself, and the old girl whirled on her axis, and pushed her way out to the stars, with a dance in her yet, wotthehell and the *think*-board was metal-and-plastic but flesh-and-blood too; part of her, of the streaming single mote which alone in this mote-filled single cell-of-Sol was bound to break out of bounds and escape to the endless entropic emptiness of Universe.

"Take a break, kid. We got a clear stretch here. Karl can take over."

He looked at the chrono, and didn't believe what he saw, and looked again. Five hours, and seventeen minutes past zero. Now aching muscles returned to sensation, and ego to Terry Carnahan.

Anita was standing beside him, one hand on a chair strap, the other held out to help.

"Whore!" he said. "Get away, bitch!"

She went away; Terry stayed where he was. What Deke could take, he could take too.

He took it for six hours more, through the last of the dust and debris of the System. He drank from the flask when it nuzzled his lips, and swallowed the pills she put in his mouth, and gave back what she needed: the readings and scannings and comps and corrections that went to the driver's seat, to the pilot's board, to Deke with the strength of ten and a tramp in his heart.

He stayed there and took it until there was no more to do. Then he reached for the straps, and her hands were already there, unfastening him.

Bitch! he thought. *Tramp! You* don't want *me!*

He let her lead him out of the room, down the ladder, through dim yellow-green, to the door where the light would be flashing red outside.

And there he stopped. There was something important to ask her, when he found out what it was, he started to smile. *Which one do you want?*

Which one? How could she possibly tell?

As well ask, *Which one needs her?*

He laughed and stepped forward . . . and the tramp was his.

WHOEVER
YOU
ARE

THIS IS A
love story. That is to say, it is a story of the greatest need
and greatest fear men know. It is also a story of conquest
and defeat, of courage and cowardice, and the heroism
that is a product of both of them. It begins in security and
isolation; it ends in victory and desecration. Whoever you
are, this story has happened to you already, and will again.
Whoever you are, however you live, you are writing the
ending to the story with every breath you take, with every
move you make.

In the cabin of the Service rocket, Scanliter Six, Sergeant Bolster and his new crewman, Pfc. Joe Fromm,
were playing checkers. It was the bored third day of a
routine one-week tour of duty on the Web, checking the
activities of the scanner-satellites that held the tight-
woven mesh of e-m-g in a hollow sphere of protective
power cast around the System.

Fromm studied the board soberly, sighed, and moved a
man into unavoidable trouble. Bolster smiled, and both
of them looked up momentarily as they heard the click
of the keys cutting tape on the receiver.

The sergeant returned his attention to the checker
board, and jumped two men before he bothered to look
up at the viewer. He saw a streak of light move upward
and across the screen in a wide expected curve, from right
to left; reached over to inspect the fresh-cut tape, and
grunted approval.

"BB-3, coming in at 26°, 13', 37", all correct," he said. "Check 'em off, Joe. "That's nine, thirty-eight, and one-oh-seven at the point of entry. All in correlation. Transmission clear. It's your move."

Fromm picked up the clipboard with the scanlite-station checkoff chart, and marked three tiny squares with his initials, almost without looking. He was still staring at the view-screen, empty now of everything but the distant specks of light that were the stars.

"Hey," Bolster said again. "It's your move."

Joe Fromm didn't even hear him. The scanner outside completed its revolution around the small ship, and . . . there it was again! The flaring trail of rockets traveled across the screen, independent of the up-and-down motion of the revolving scanner.

The sergeant grunted again. "What's the matter? Didn't you ever see one home before?"

"That's the first," Fromm said without turning. "Shouldn't we be recording the tape?"

"Not yet." Bolster surveyed the checker board sadly; he'd have a king on the next move . . . if Fromm ever made another move. "All we got now is radar-recog. Then . . . there you are . . ." He nodded at the renewed clacking of the keys. "That'll be the code-dope coming in. Then we wait till after it hits detection, and we get the last OK, before we send the tape to the Post."

He explained it all dutifully just the same. It used to be when they sent a new man out, they at least took him on a practice tour first. "Look, make a move will you? You got a whole year here to sit and look at 'em come in."

With difficulty, the Pfc. took his eyes off the viewer, touch a piece on the board at random, and pushed it forward, leaving Bolster with the choice of a three-man jump to nowhere, or the one-man jump that would net him his king. The private leaned forward to finger the tape as it emerged from the receiver, reading off the replies to code-dope demands, and signal responses, with a certain reverent intensity. "Did you ever see an illegal entry?" he asked. "I mean an attempt? Somebody told me there was one on this sect . . ."

At that instant the BB-3 hit the detector field awaiting it at the point of entry on the Web, and generated mechanical panic in an entire sequence of scanlite instruments. Synchronized pulses from the three scanlite stations circling the point of entry transmitted their frustration in the face of the unprecedented and unpredicted; and the tape in the cabin of Scanliter Six vibrated out of the recorder under the furious impact of the chattering keys.

Alarm bells began to shrill: first in the small cabin, directly over the sergeant's head; then in similar cabins on four other Scanliter rockets within range; finally, about two minutes later, in the Exec Office at Phobos Post, which was the nearest Solar Defense base to the point of entry at the time.

Pfc. Joe Fromm stopped his hesitant query in mid-word, feeling vaguely guilty for having brought the subject up. Sergeant Bolster knocked over the checker board reaching for the tape. He read it, paled visibly, passed it across to the private, and started transmitting to the Post almost at the same instant.

On Phobos, a Signal Tech. depressed three levers on his switchboard before he stopped to wonder what was wrong. Green alarm meant emergency calls to the O.D., Psychofficer, and P.R. Chief. The Tech. sent out the summons, then stopped to read the tape.

DYTEKTR FYLD RYPORT: BB-3 EM RADA-SHNZ INDKAT ALYN LIF—RYPYT ALYN LIF UBORD. RYPT: DYTEKTR FYLD RYPORT VIA SKANLITS 9-38-107 TU SKANLITR 6 SHOZ NO UMN LIF UBORD BB-3.
                                        BOLSTER, SGT/SKNR 6

By the time the Phobos Post Commander got up from his dinner table, the Psychofficer put down the kitten he was playing with, and the Public Relations Deputy pushed back the stool at her dressing table, the crews of all five

Scanliters within range of the point of entry, as well as the Signals Tech. on Phobos, knew all the pertinent details of what had occurred.

The *Baby Byrd III*, a five-man starscout, under command of Captain James Malcolm, due back after almost a full year out of System, had approched a point of entry just outside the orbit of Saturn on the electromagneto-gravitic Web of force that surrounded the Solar System. It had signalled the correct radar recognition pattern, and replied to the challenge of the scanlite stations circling the point of entry with the anticipated code responses. Accordingly, the point had been softened to permit entry of the ship, and a standard detector set up around the soft spot.

Thus far, it was routine homecoming for a starscout. It was only when the BB-3 entered the detector field that the automatics on the scanner-satellite stations began to shrill the alarms for human help. The field registered no human electro-magnetic emanations on board the BB-3. The e-m pattern it got was undoubtedly alive . . . and just as undeniably alien.

For the third time in the history of the Web, an attempt at entry had been made by unauthorized aliens; and those aliens were apparently in sole possession of a Solar starscout. The third attempt . . . and the third failure: the BB-3 was already secured in a slightly intensified smaller sphere of the same e-m-g mesh that made up the Web, suspended at midpoint between the three circling scanlite stations.

Eternal vigilance is most assuredly the price of the peace of the womb. The membrane of force that guarded the System from intrusion had, in turn, to be guarded and maintained by the men who lived within it. The scanner-satellites were as nearly infallible as a machine can be; they might have run effectively for centuries on their own very slowly diminishing feedback-power systems. But man's security was too precious a thing to trust entirely to the products of man's ingenuity. Each year a new group of the System's youth was called to Service, and at the end of the year, a few were chosen from among the volunteers to man the Scanliters that serviced the satellite stations which comprised the Web.

For even the most adventurous of youths, one further year of Scanliting was usually enough; they came back from their fifty tours Outside prepared to keep their feet on solid ground, and to forget the brief experience of facing the unknown. But each year, too, there were a few of them who learned to crave the intoxication of danger, who could no longer be content to settle back into the warm security of the System. It was these warped veterans of the Web who became Byrdmen.

Secure within the womb-enclosure of the Web, five billion Solar citizens could wreak their wills upon their little worlds, and carry on the ever more complex design for nourishment of all the intra-System castes and categories.

Outside, the emissaries of mankind streaked through the heavens on their chariots of fire, spreading the Solar culture through galactic space, spawning the seeds of men between the stars. First went the Baby Byrds, to scout new lands beyond the farthest outposts; then the Byrds, with their full complements of scientists, and giant laboratories, to test the promise of the newly-charted planets; and after them, the giant one-way starships went.

Somehow there were always just enough bold desperate souls, yearning for danger and ready to die for a dream, to fill the human cargo-couches of the colony ships: the Mayflowers and Livingstons and Columbos that left the safety of the Web forever to fix new germ-cells of humanity on far-flung planets in the speckled skies.

Inside the Web, on four inhabited planets and half a thousand habitable asteroids, men lived in the light of the sun by day, and drew their warmth and power from it. By night, they turned to rest at peace; each one under his own sector of the high-domed sky, the hollow sphere of force through which no alien source of light could penetrate and still retain identity.

The Web glowed always with the mingled and diffracted energy of all the universe Outside; no photon passed its portals, no smallest particle of energy came through without the necessary pause for hail-and-password that maintained the calm security of the Web's inner light.

Scanliter Six was already proceeding at full speed toward the trapped BB, acting on normal emergency procedures, when the keys taped out the order from Commander Harston on Phobos post to do just that. No stars showed on the viewer; they had stopped the rotation of the scanner and the screen held a steady picture of the three Scanlite stations with a fuzzy hump in the center that was too bright to look at comfortably. Scanner rays could not possibly penetrate the thick field that held the BB-3 suspended in the Web.

"Well," Bolster said sourly. "Here's your chance to be a hero, kid."

Joe Fromm knew it was childish of him to be excited. He tried not to look interested. "Yeah?" he said.

"Yeah. What happens now is, we get there and code in that the situation is as reported. Then the brass has a conference and they decide somebody has got to investigate, so they ask for volunteers. We're the laddies on the spot. The other boys are all on Stand-by according to this. . . ."

He waved the orders tape at Fromm, who caught it and read it through carefully.

"And if we were on Stand-by instead of Proceed, you know what we'd be doing right now?" the sergeant went on, enjoying his own discomfort as loudly as possible. "I'll tell you what. We'd be standing all right, right smack where we were when the tape came in. Not one second closer."

"Stand-by is supposed to mean that you get into the best position for observation," the Pfc. recited.

"Sure. The best position for observation, kid, is in-scan and out of blowup range. So you take your choice: you stay where you are when the tape comes in, or you back out as far as you can and stay in-scan. Anyhow, we're the boys on the spot, see? They're going to want a volunteer to board the Beebee, and I got a hunch," he finished with a faint note of hope, "that I might come out of this in one piece just on account of you are probably going to want to be a hero."

"Could be," Fromm said nonchalantly. "You're senior; after all, it's your privilege."

He was delighted that he managed to keep a poker face throughout the statement

Joe Fromm stepped out of the airlock into space, and let himself float free, orienting, for a slow count of five. He had done it a hundred times and more in drill, but it felt different now. As in the drill, he made a routine extra check of his equipment: tank, jetter, axe, welder, magno-grapple mechitape recorder, (no radio in an insul-suit), knife, gun, signal mirror, medikit. All OK.

He set the jet at gentle and squirted off toward the glowing ball of force that held the starscout. Two more squirts, and he was as close as he could get. He flashed the mirror twice at Bolster in the Scanliter, to start the passageway in the sphere opening. This was the last contact till he came out again. If he . . .

If I come out again . . . he thought the whole phrase through deliberately, and was surprised at the way his mind accepted the possibility, and dismissed it. He felt tremendously alive, almost as if each separate cell was tingling with some special vigor and awareness. And in the center of it all, in some hidden part of himself, he was dead calm, almost amused. Was this what they called courage?

He flashed the mirror again. Bolster was certainly taking his time. All he had to do was throw a switch. Fromm began flashing angry code with the mirror and kept it up, knowing Bolster couldn't answer and rejoicing in the knowledge, until he saw the opening appear in the ball of force, and begin to expand.

Then he realized it wasn't simply throwing a switch. Once the passageway-mechanism was put into operation, it had to keep going on its own, opening and closing at intervals so as to permit him egress, and still not let enough e-m-g through in either direction to disturb the power-stasis inside. It took only a little bit of computer work . . . but quite a bit more intricate checking of the relays, to make certain the automatics would not fail.

He had to hold himself back to keep from diving through as soon as the hole was as big as his suit . . . but he waited, as he had been trained to do, until it stopped enlarging. The computer knew better than he did how much space he needed.

Then he squirted forward and through. The BB looked strange, hanging there in the middle of nothing, with an air of polite impatience, waiting to finish its passage into the System.

Joe grinned, and duly spoke his thought out loud for the record. "Every single thing that passes through your head," they'd said over and over again in school. "When you're on any kind of solo operation, you want to be sure the guy who takes over knows everything you did, no matter how crazy it seems. An idea that doesn't connect for you could make sense to him."

So Joe Fromm told the mechitape attachment on his suit that the starscout looked impatient. He kept talking, describing his actions and thoughts and emotions, as he approached the ship cautiously, and opened the outer lock door. More waiting, and he informed the tape that the air lock was in operating condition.

Then he was in the ship, and omitted to mention in his running commentary that he was scared silly. Down the corridor . . . open the cabin doors one at a time . . . empty, empty . . . not empty. Go on in, Joe; he's out cold; couldn't hurt a fly.

"One of the aliens is in this cabin. This is the third door I have opened, second cabin to the right going down the corridor from the lock to Control . . . he's either dead or unconscious . . . hope they're all like that . . . he's *big* . . . hope they're not all like that. Maybe ten feet tall, sort of curled up on the bunk, might have been asleep." Might still be, might wake up.

He gulped and decided he'd better put it on record. "Might still . . ." No, that was foolish. These characters had registered e.m. radiations on the instruments in the stations. They couldn't stay conscious inside the e.m.g.

field without insul-suits. Anything strong enough to stop a BB in its tracks would stop a man too.

But it's not a man; it's . . . "It's definitely humanoid . . . hard to believe any alien creatures could evolve so much like humans. No tenacles, nothing like that. Arms and hands look like ours . . . fingers too. He's wearing some kind of robe . . . hard to get it loose with these gloves on, can't see the legs for sure, but the arms are human all right. Face is different, something funny about the mouth, sort of pursed-up-looking. Closed, can't see the inside . . . guess I can try and open it . . . no, later, maybe. I better take a look around. Anyhow, this guy is a lot like you and me only almost twice as big. Not very hairy, dark skin, big black eyes . . . how can anything that's not human have eyes that look at you like that, even when he's out cold? I don't know . . . going out now, next cabin, second door on the left . . .

"Here's another one . . . on the floor this time, kind of crumpled up . . . must have been standing when the field hit, and fell down. Nothing new here . . . wait a minute, this fella must have cut his hand on something when he fell . . . yeah, there's an open locker door, with an edge. Blood is dried, looks like it's a lot darker than ours, but it's crazy how human it looks anyhow . . . Going out again now . . . in the corridor, no more doors here . . ."

There were two more of them in the control room: one strapped in the pilot's seat, squeezed in really; he just about could make it. The other was slumped over the solar analog computer.

"Looks like he was checking the landing data," Fromm reported. "These guys sure were confident. Two of 'em off shift when they were coming in, and everything set for a normal landing. Didn't they figure on any trouble at all? They should have realized they couldn't just sit down on one of our planets. Hell, they knew about the Web; they gave the code-dope straight, and they decelerated to approach, and had the correct angle . . . I don't get it . . . Here goes once around the room now. I will check all instruments.

"Starting from the door, and turning right: Star-chart

microviewer intact and operating, films filed properly, I think. Won't take time to check them all now, but they look right. . . . Radio desk appears in normal condition for use, can't test. . . . Space suit locker is full of strange stuff, will come back to examine. . . . analog comps come next; this guy is sprawled all over them. . . ."

He followed his nose around the cylindrical room, till he came back to the door again. Everything was, or seemed to be, in good working order. A few adjustments had been made in levers and handholds, to fit the aliens' larger hands; otherwise, virtually nothing had been touched except for normal use.

"Okay, I guess I better start on the locker now. . . ." But he didn't want to; he felt suddenly tired. Not scared any more . . . maybe that was it. Now he knew he was safe, and there weren't any booby traps or anything seriously wrong, he was feeling the strain. Let Bolster do some work too, he thought angrily, and almost said it out loud for the tape. Then he realized that his sudden pique was really just weariness, and at the same time he became acutely aware of hunger and an even more pressing biological urge. Time to go home, Joe. Always leave the party early, that's how to stay popular.

He ought at least to get the robe off one of the creatures first, and make sure about their anatomy, but he had an odd reluctance to do it. They were too human . . . it seemed as if it wasn't fair somehow to go poking around under their clothes.

Hell! Let Bolster do it! He left the ship.

Alone in the Scanliter, Joe Fromm played his mechi-tape into the permanent recorder, and turned up the volume so he could hear it himself, and get everything clear for his report to Phobos. Some of the stuff sounded crazy, but he could tell what part was fact and what was just his own imagination. He chewed on a pencil end, and occasionally noted down something he should be sure to remember.

Altogether, composing the report was more painful than visiting the ship had been. He had just started putting it

onto the transmitter when he saw the indicater for the
outer lock light up. Bolster sure hadn't stayed on that ship
long! He felt better now about coming back himself.

The sergeant came inside shedding his insul-suit, and
bursting with excitement.

"You should of looked in that locker, kid!" He was
triumphant. "Anyway, it's a good thing for me you didn't.
This is the kind of good luck bonuses are made of." He
removed an envelope carefully from the storage pocket
on the outside of the suit. "Got your stuff in yet? I want
to shoot this to them fast!"

"I just started . . ." Fromm said.

"Well, we'll flash this, and you can finish up afterwards."

He handed the envelope to the younger man, and
started climbing out of the leg pieces of the suit. "Go on!
Read it, man!"

Fromm opened the flap and unfolded a piece of official
Service stationary. To whom it may concern; it said on
top, and then right underneath: To the Staff Officers of
Solar Defense:

"The other men have asked me to write this message,
and I guess I can do it all right, but I'm afraid I'll
have to be pretty informal. I've tried to write it up in
military report style, only it's just not the kind of thing
that Service language fits.

"For one thing, the very first line of the report form
stopped me, because we don't know where we are. Only
the Captain knew our orders and he's dead now, and we
couldn't find his log, or any of his papers, anywhere in
the ship.

"We've set a course for the big fellas by backtracking
on the analog comps. That means it will take them almost
as long to get back as it took us to get there, but that's
just as well, because it will bring them in about the time
our tour is due up, and maybe that'll make it easier for
them to get in.

"We've done our best to explain to them all the dangers
involved—not being sure of the course, even, and being
pretty sure you folks won't let them through. But we can't

talk to them as easy as they talk to us. We can get over general ideas all right, and any kind of thought that has a solid object nearby to attach to, but the idea of people, of humans that is, not wanting to let them into the System—well, even if we talked the same language . . . that is, if they talked a language at all that we could learn . . . I don't think they could understand that idea.

"I'm not going to try to tell you anything about them because if they get far enough to show you this, they can explain everything themselves. This message is just to let you know that the four of us are here, safe and sound, and staying behind of our own free will. Since Captain Malcolm's suicide, there's nobody to order us home, and we like it here. Besides, there isn't room enough in the BB for more than five people—humans, I mean—or four of them (they need more food). And they want to send four along on the trip; I think they picked out their leading scientists in different fields, so they can get as much information as possible, and be able to answer your questions.

"I don't know. Probably a Psychofficer or some of our scientists will be able to communicate better with them on this kind of thing. We get along fine for everyday purposes, but you see, I'm not even sure what kind of scientists they're sending.

"The only thing the others and I are sure of, and that's what this message is for, is that you can trust these big fellas up to the limit. They've treated us fine, and they . . . well, it's a funny way to put it, but "like" isn't strong enough . . . they just seem to love everybody, humans as well as their own kind.

"We will wait here for further orders. You can probably figure out where we are from the analog comp records.

"Respectfully yours,
"George Gentile, Byrdman 1st Class,
and on behalf of
"Johann Grauber By/2
Tsin Lao-Li, By/2
Arne Carlsen, By/3."

"I did a tour of duty with Jim Malcolm once," the Commander said slowly. "He was a pretty good guy. I . . . liked him. It's hard to think of him committing suicide. I wish this Gentile had been a little more specific."

Lucille Ardin, Public Relations Deputy at Phobos Post, skimmed the message tape rapidly, and passed it along to the Psychofficer. She cocked one feathery eyebrow cynically. "These boys just don't make sense," she said. "They've been sold something all right . . . but what?"

The Commander shook his head, waiting for Dr. Schwartz to finish reading. "Well, Bob?" he said, as soon as the Psychofficer looked up. "What do you think?"

"I'd like to see that log," Schwartz said thoughtfully.

"So would I!" Commander William Hartson had earned his position as Assistant Chief of Staff for Solar Defense. He was that rare thing: an officer admired equally by the general public and by the men who worked under him. At sixty-eight years of age, he was still in the prime of health and vitality—but old enough to have seen his fill of violence, danger, and death. He was decisive in action; but a decision involving the lives of others would be made with care.

Bob Schwartz had worked with Hartson long enough to understand these things. "This Captain . . . ?" he asked, "Malcolm? Would you say he was . . . well, a fairly typical line officer?"

The Commander permitted himself a faint smile. "'Trying to figure the 'military mind' again, Bob? As a matter of fact, I think Jim Malcolm is—was one of the few officers who'd fit your picture pretty well. Courage, devotion, precision—a stubborn s.o.b., who went by the rule book himself and figured everybody else could do at least as much . . . but the kind who'd lay down his life for his Service without thinking twice. It's just suicide that doesn't make sense. . . ."

Harston's voice broke off, and for a moment the only sound in the room was the shuffling of paper. Schwartz still held the message tape, running it through his fingers as if the feel of it would somehow help him to understand its meaning better. Lucy Ardin pushed away the pad on which she'd been scribbling Hartson's explanation of the forcesphere that was holding the BB-3 captive and its alien crew unconscious.

"God, what a story!" she whispered reverently into the silence. She ground out a half-smoked cigarette in the Commander's big ash-tray, and stood up; the silver-sequinned dinner gown in which she'd answered the alarm glittered painfully under the overhead light. It was entirely typical of Lucy that when the call-bell rang in her bedroom, she had pushed back the stool from her dressing table without taking even the extra instant's time to complete the slash of crimson on her lips. Then picking up the portfolio that was always ready for use, she had arrived at the Exec Office, with the lipsticking finished en route, within seconds after the two men who lived on the Post.

"All right," she said briskly. "What happens now? We stitch up some six-tentacled strait-jackets and make our visitors nice and safe, then we take the field off and haul 'em down? Where to? What do we do with them afterwards? Who gets to interview them?"

The Psychofficer looked up sharply, and Hartson chuckled. "Relax, Bob. I'm afraid it's our baby all the way down the line. I wish I was looking forward to it like you two are. I have a hunch it may turn out to be something of a mess. . . . The aliens, by the way, are humanoid, Miss Ardin. Perhaps you'd like to see the tape again? I believe there's a detailed description . . . hey Bob? You're done with it, aren't you?"

"Sorry." Schwartz handed it to the girl, and snapped out of his abstracted mood. "Is it safe to leave them in the stasis a little longer, Bill?" he asked.

"Can't say for sure. With humans, twelve hours doesn't do any harm. These fellas may be dead already for all we know. Best we can do is assume they react like us."

"It seems to me that log must be somewhere on the ship," the Psychofficer said. "If there's time, I think it might be a good idea to try and find it—before we decide anything. A man like Malcolm would have made sure the papers were safe, if he had any way to do it at all."

"You're right." Hartson, too, came up from his reflections and sprang into action. "You're damned right! If it's there we can find it. And if we can't—well, that's an answer too!"

Joe Fromm went back to the BB-3 with two other men from the stand-in Scanliters that had now been ordered up to assist. Between them, they searched the Byrd from nose to nozzles, and behind a panel in the electrical repair cabinet, they found the ship's papers: charts, orders, and the missing log.

Fromm took time to open the log and look at the last page: he hardly had to struggle with his conscience at all over it. Under the dateline, in neat typing, it said:

"Carlsen should have been back an hour ago. Under the circumstances, that means they've got him too. My error was in not leaving after I talked to Tsin last week. Three of us could have brought the ship back. Alone, I don't believe I can do it.

"I have considered taking off anyhow, simply in order to make certain the natives do not gain any further knowledge of the ship. My only choices now are betrayal or ¹f-destruction, and between these two, I am afraid I have no real choice. I must therefore pick the most effective means of suicide, and after giving the matter careful thought, have determined that a systematic destruction of the control room is a wiser procedure than the complete removal of the ship from the planet.

"By following this course of action, I can at least hope that a future expedition, or perhaps even a rescue-ship, will find this log and understand the danger here.

"This evening, I shall have my last supper in style. Tomorrow, I shall finish the dismantling of the controls, and hide this book, together with the more important of the ship's papers . . . and may God have mercy on my soul!"

Below that, in almost equally neat and legible a script, were two paragraphs.

"Once more I have delayed too long. Gentile, my firstclassman, is at the outer lock now, and he has three of the natives with him. Apparently they now have him sufficiently under control so that he will do for them what they have not dared to do for themselves. They are coming into the ship.

"I expect they are coming for me, and I cannot risk exposing myself to their control. I know too much that they can use. The work of dismantling the controls is barely started; I'm afraid the enlisted men can still repair it readily, but none of them, after all, even know where we are; the star-charts and orders will be hidden with this log. I can only hope the papers remain hidden until the right people come to find them."

Underneath, there was a careful signature: "James Malcolm, Captain, Solar Byrd Service, in command *Baby Byrd III*," and in parenthesis below that, one word of macabre humor, "(deceased)."

They ordered Scanliter Six down to Phobos Post, to bring in the papers of the BB-3. There was too much material to transmit by radio.

Bolster grinned and slapped his Pfc. on the back. "We're both a couple of bloomin' heroes," he said. "Just the kind of a hero I like to be. Some other guys'll be around when they decide to blast that *Baby*, and you and me can watch it all from the Post."

"Blast it?" Joe looked up from the log, holding his finger in the page. "You're kidding. Why would they . . ."

"Brother, you got the reason wrapped around your finger. One look at that, and they'll blow those babies clear back to where they come from! You can take a chance on a guy who fights fair, but these fellas—"

"How do you know they're fighting us?" Fromm demanded. "You saw the Byrdman's note, the one you brought in. . . . This guy Malcolm was off his rocker!"

"Well, I'll buy that one, too. You can't tell with the brass when they get an idea in their heads. But look, kid, you gotta grow up some. That note I brought in—it's pretty easy to get a guy to write something like that if you got him hypnotized to start with, and you're twice his size anyhow—not to mention there being a whole planetful of your kind and only four of his. I can tell you anyhow, that's how the brass'll see it. Solar Defense doesn't take chances."

"Did you read what it says here?" Fromm insisted. "The part where Malcolm tells us about talking to Tsin? It just doesn't make sense to take it the way he did. He was space-happy, that's all. The Commander isn't going to swallow this stuff."

"You wait and see," the sergeant said again. "And when you do, you're gonna be awful glad you're down there instead of here."

"I . . . look, I know this sounds crazy . . ." Fromm put the log down finally, and blurted out the rest of it. "I'd like to stick around. If anybody goes back out there, I want a chance to take another look at those guys. You think you could take somebody from one of the other ships down with you, and leave me here?"

"It not only sounds crazy," Bolster said. "It is crazy. But it's your body, son. You want to stick around, you can bet nobody else does." He shook his head uncomprehendingly, and began punching out a message to Scanliter Twelve, where Chan Lal would jump at the chance to change spots with his weakwitted Pfc.

"I ordered him to return to ship immediately. He refused. His exact words, insofar as I recall them, were, 'Captain, I wish I could do as you desire me to—or even better that I could convince you to come with me and visit our friends. They are our friends. If you would give them a chance to talk with you, I think you might understand better. It is hard to explain with just words. But I simply cannot go back now. (Emphasis is mine . . . JM) You are a married man, sir. Perhaps I might feel differently if there were some love waiting for me at home too. But I am young and not yet married, and . . .'"

"I broke in here, thinking that I might be able to use persuasion, where authority had failed. I pointed out that there was very little likelihood he would ever be married, if I decided to take up the ship, abandoning him and Gentile on the planet—as of course, I have every right to do in view of their outright insubordination. The natives here, for all their startlingly humanoid appearance, are twice our size, and are almost certainly not suitable for breeding, from a purely biologic viewpoint.

"He replied quite earnestly that he hoped I would not take that drastic step . . . that he did not wish to remain permanently among the natives, but that he felt he 'had to' stay long enough to become fully acquainted with them and with their way of life, and to 'be healed of all the hurts and scars of a lifetime in the System.'

"The conversation went on for some time, but the parts I have already recorded contain the gist of it. There was one thing Tsin said, however, that I feel should be included here, along with the train of thought that followed it. If anything should happen to me or to my ship, I suspect it will in some way be connected with my low susceptibility to the emotional point he seemed to be trying to make.

"Tsin reminded me, during the conversation, of a story I have always considered rather bathetic: that of the little orphan girl, in the days before the creches, who threw a note over the high wall of the 'orphanage' saying: 'Whoever you are, I love you.'

"This anecdote, I gathered, was supposed to define for me the nature of the emotional 'healing' he was receiving at the hands—or I suppose I should say the minds—of the natives.

"This particular bit of bathos has been annoying me for years. I have had the story related to me at least three times previously, always to illustrate some similarly obscure emotional point. And I have always wondered afterwards what the end of the story might have been.

"Now it seems very important to be able to forsee the results of the child's action. What happened when the note was picked up and read? And why did the child write it?

"It is this last question, I think, that bothers me the most. A sentimentalist might answer that she meant it, but I find this unlikely. At best, I believe, she meant that she hoped whoever found it would love her; and that is the very best interpretation I can put on it. It seems even more likely that her motive was even more specific: if she threw such *billet doux* over the wall regularly, I should think eventually one of the sentimentalists would have found it, made some response, and provided the means for her to get over the orphanage wall into the world outside.

"The natives here have a fairly highly-developed technology, and quite obviously a very highly-developed psychology or mental science of some sort. They are telepaths, after all. And they have taken no pains to conceal from us their interest in acquiring a means of space travel.

"There is nothing to pin down, no way to make certain of their real attitudes towards us. They have greeted us warmly, and have done nothing to indicate any hostility or to harm us in any way—nothing but walk off with two of my crew in an apparently friendly fashion.

"Perhaps the wisest course of action would be to leave now, while I still have two men on board. But it is a hard decision to make—to maroon two of my men on an alien planet.

"If I believed for a moment that Gentile and Tsin are responsible for their own actions, I should not hesitate to make that decision. But their behavior is so entirely 'out of character' that I can see no explanation except that they are acting under some form of hypnotic control. As I see it, my duty is to make every effort, including main force, to return them to the ship before I leave."

Hartson read it for the fourth time, and slapped the typescript down on the desk. "I . . . hell, Jim Malcolm was a friend of mine! How can I tell? It sounds like him . . . sure! It sounds like every report he ever wrote, except where it sounds like him being pie-eyed in a bull-session."

He sat down, and let the blank bewilderment he felt show in his eyes as he faced the Psychofficer. "Well, what do you say? I can't decide this one by myself."

Courtesy turned him, halfway through the question to face the PR Chief on the other side of the desk. Courtesy, and common sense, both. Officially, Lucy's job was just to get out the news—or to keep it in, as seemed wisest. The catch was in that last phrase. In practice, she was both public censor and interpreter-at-large for the Post; and her Civil Service appointment made her the only authority on Phobos who was independent of the Service.

The Commander had been dealing with the P.R. Bureau long enough so that in six months at the Post, Lucy had never yet had any cause to remove her velvet glove. It was easy to forget sometimes about the iron beneath it; one might almost think that she forgot herself.

"I'll check to Doctor Schwartz," she demurred now.

Schwartz managed a smile. "Will you please stop being polite?" he asked. "You've got an opinion. Let's hear it." She hesitated, and he added: "I don't even like what I'm thinking. I better think it a little more before I say it."

"All right." Her voice was controlled, but her eyes gleamed with excitement. She was talking at Schwartz, almost ignoring the Commander. "I think these fellas have the biggest thing since e-m-g. It's the one thing we haven't been able to crack at all; you know it as well as I do. They've got the unbeatable weapon—the psychological weapon. You can't fight 'em, because you don't want to. People call modern P.R. mass hypnotism, but the techniques we've got are child's play compared to what these guys can do. They've got the real thing. The question is, can we get it away from them? Has Psych Section got any way of handling something this hot?"

"I take it," Hartson put in drily, "that you are convinced of the accuracy of Captain Malcolm's interpretation of the events?"

She looked puzzled. "Why . . . yes. How else can you explain it? Has there ever been a case of desertion like that before?"

"Never," he said crisply, and turned to the Psychofficer again. "All right, Bob. You've had some time now. Say your piece."

"Let me start this way" Schwartz said hesitantly. "I think Lucy is right on one respect anyway . . . what they've got is an irresistible weapon. If it is a weapon. But to accept that idea, we'd have to presuppose the existence of a war, or at least hostility between them and us. There's a verse that's been running through my head for the last hour. I'm sorry, Bill, to be so roundabout. Just try to put up with me a few minutes, will you? I can't quite remember the whole thing, but it's about an 'enemy' who 'drew a circle to keep me out.' Then there's a line I remember clearly: 'But love and I knew better. We drew a circle to bring him in.' You see what I'm driving at? Certainly our basic attitude toward any alien is potientially hostile. They are guilty until proven innocent."

"We've been all over that ground, Bob," Hartson broke in. "I know your opinion, and you ought to know mine by now. I don't like it either, but it's the reason why we have been consistently successful in such contacts."

"Consistently victorious, I'd say. All right, let's just put it that I am emotionally more inclined to accept Gentile's attitude than Malcolm's. I see no evidence to support the view that these people are using a hypnotic weapon; it is at least as likely that the feeling they projected at our men was honest and uncalculated. Why not assume for a moment that the occupants of that ship really are four of their leading scientists, sent here to exchange knowledge with us?"

"You've got a point there," Lucy Ardin said unexpectedly. "An act of aggression against these four could make trouble if they were on the level to start with. I think it gets down to a good old-fashioned problem in shielding. Has Psych Section got any way of handling these boys if we bring them in, Doc?"

He considered for a moment.

"That depends. We've got anti-hypnotics, and we've got personnel specially trained against susceptibility to hypnosis. But the Beebee had the same drugs, and should have had some trained personnel too. There's a point, Bill. I'd like to see the basic psych ratings on all five of those men, if you can get 'em. Especially Malcolm's. I could get the papers myself," he added, smiling weakly, "Through channels, it wouldn't take more than three or four weeks. Can you get 'em fast?"

"I can try." Hartson jumped at the chance for concrete action. He rang for an aide, and scribbled an order to Records in his own handwriting. "Put this on the facscan," he said briskly, "and give it a top-rush priority. I think I see what you're getting at, Bob," he said, as the door closed behind the uniformed girl. "I remember I was kind of surprised myself when I heard Jim had gone into the Byrd Service. Couldn't imagine him going Outside voluntarily. He was an Earthman all the way through. Why he didn't even believe Marsmen were really human. Is that what you wanted to know?"

"Part of it. That much was pretty clear in his report. I want to know the comparative resistance of the crew members to hypnosis and what the other men's attitudes were toward alien life—things like that."

"I thought all Byrdmen had to pass standardized tests for that," the PR Chief said, just a little sharply.

"They do. At least, the enlisted men do. But there's still a range of individual variation. And officers . . . well, they have a tough time getting enough men to command the Beebees. I think just about any regular line officer who volunteered would pass the test. . . ."

He looked to Hartson for confirmation, and got a reluctant nod; then he went on. "Even with the men, it depends where they took their tests. That'll show on the papers. Psych Section isn't too—efficient—in some spots."

"I'll bear that in mind," Lucy said tautly. "But I'd still like to know just how much Psych Section right here is equipped to do. You say you've got the drugs and the personnel, Doctor. All right, then, if the Commander brings these fellows in alive, can you handle them? If you can't . . ." She shrugged.

"That depends." The Psychofficer declined the challenge of her tone and went on deliberately: "We can handle it all right . . . if it's as simple a thing as hypnosis. It happens that I don't believe Captain Malcolm was right about that. I can tell better after I see his psych ratings. . . ."

"All right! Then I take it we're going to sit around here for the next few hours waiting to see what the tests say? That gives you a little more time to make up your mind. Well, if I'm going to spend the night here, I'd like to be a little more comfortable. Do you mind if I run home for a change of clothes while we're waiting, Commander?"

Hartson eyed the shimmering stiffness of her dinner gown unhappily. "I'm sorry, Miss Ardin. I hope you'll understand. This qualifies as a Major Policy decision, and I'm afraid I'll have to ask you not to leave until we are finished with whatever we decide."

She shrugged again, and sat down. "Could I have a typer then? I could be getting some of my story into shape."

Schwartz laughed. From the vantage point of the smoking jacket and carpet slippers in which he'd answered the emergency call, he said easily, "Bill, couldn't you order something from Supply for the lady? S.I. coveralls, or something like that? It might make a difference in our decision if she could be more comfortable."

"I can do that," Hartson said shortly. "And of course you may have any equipment you wish, Miss Ardin."

"Thank you, Commander," she said, too sweetly. "I'm sure it will help. I wonder if perhaps we could facilitate matters by sending for the doctor's uniform too? If I'm to be made more flexible, I suspect a change of clothes might make him more decisive."

Hartson grinned. "She's got a point there, Bob," he said mildly.

"All right!" The Psychofficer stood up abruptly, paced the length of the small room, and wheeled to face them. "All right, I'll tell you what I think. I think the human race is too damn scared and too damn hungry to be able to face this thing. Hungry for security, for reassurance, for comfort—for love. And scared! Scared of anything different, anything Outside, anything one degree more intense than the rules allow.

"Also—pardon my bluntness, Bill—I think Captain Malcolm's reaction was typical of all that's sickest in our System. The very fact that we are seriously sitting here considering how much of a menace these four individuals represent—four humanoid beings, who come armed with nothing but a message of love! That very fact—that we sit and stew over it, I mean—makes them dangerous.

"You want to know what I think? I think what they've got—whether it's a weapon or a natural way of life, whether it's hypnotism or open-hearted honesty, or anything else, is—not unbeatable, not ultimate, not any of the other adjectives that've been thrown around here tonight but, specifically, irresistible.

"I think all of us—you, Bill, wanting to do the 'blameless' thing—and you, suffering through hours of torment in those ridiculous clothes because they're supposed to make you 'attractive'—and maybe me most of all, hating to say what I know because it's brutal—all of us and the rest of the System too, have one crying need that the lousy culture we've made for ourselves can't possibly fulfill.

"We want love. We need love. Every poor blessed damned soul among us. And we need it so much, it can be used as a weapon against us!

"Understand, please, just because it's important to me to have it on the record, that I don't for a moment believe it's hypnotism they're using. I think they mean it. But . . ."

"Well, at last!" Lucy Ardin sighed and moved a tense finger for the first time since he'd started talking. "Then you think you can handle it?"

Schwartz stared at her in amazement. "Didn't you hear anything I said? No. No, I don't think I can handle it, or that anybody else can. I don't believe it's hypnosis, but I can't see that that matters. Or rather, I might feel more at ease about it if I could believe that.

"Damn it, Bill, I hate this! I want you to understand clearly that the advice I am giving you is against my own inclinations and instincts. Now look: if it is to be regarded as a weapon—and I see no other way we may regard it from the point of view of Solar Defense—then it is irresistible. There is no way to tie or bind the minds of these—people—except by keeping them unconscious, which would automatically defeat any purpose of investigation."

He picked up his copy of the summary and excerpts from the log, riffled through the pages, and threw it down again, sadly. "Bill, I'd give all my ratings, and ten

years off my life for the chance to talk to those guys myself, and find out . . . but my advice as an officer of Solar
Defense is that we have no choice but to destroy the
aliens before they regain consciousness."

Both the others were on their feet as he finished.

"God damn it, Bob!" Hartson shouted. "You can't
just . . ."

"Don't you see?" Lucy Ardin's crisp voice cut in. "All
he's saying is he doesn't know; none of us know, and I
want to find out! I'm not scared of it. Maybe you need
love that bad, Psychofficer, but I don't!" She sat down
again, triumphant and breathless.

The Commander ignored her. "Is that your last word,
Bob? Shall I take that as your decision?"

"I'm afraid so, Bill. You heard Lucy just now. Remember what Malcolm was wondering, about the end of the
story of the little orphan girl? That's one answer. In terms
of the little girl, it would mean that whoever found the
note took it back inside and told the authorities that one
of their children was writing dirty notes—so the kid could
be investigated. That's just one ending. There are lots of
others, but don't forget the one he was afraid of. Don't
forget all the sentimentalists—like me for instance. If I
were to forget my duty as an officer of the Service, I
would want nothing more than to get the little girl out of
the orphanage, just so she could love them.

"And don't forget, either, that there would be any
number of different answers besides. And that everyone
would feel strongly about his own solution. You have your
choice, Commander. You can destroy them in the name
of Security and Safety—or you can risk a System-wide
civil war, and total 'conquest' by an alien race. What'll
you have?"

Commander Hartson smiled wryly. "I'll take vanilla,"
he said distinctly, and rang for an aide. The uniformed
girl appeared in the doorway. "Jenny," he said, "I want
orders typed up for countersigning to arrange all details
for the moving of the Baby Byrd III to Deimos Isolation
Post immediately. The ship will be piloted by Pfc.
Joseph Fromm, now aboard the Scanliter Twelve. We

will want a continuous radio report from the pilot starting with his entry into the ship.

"Separate orders are to go to Scanliters Seventeen and Twenty-two, to follow the BB-3 in with all artillery on the ready. They are to maintain radio silence, with vocal reception open. Private Fromm is to know nothing of the ready-fire orders. The word "apple" will be the signal to fire, if I decide it is necessary to destroy the ship. Is that all clear?"

"Yes, sir."

The door closed quietly behind her, and Bob Schwartz stood up and walked around the desk to shake the Commander's hand.

"They say you're a great man, Bill," he said quietly. "I'm beginning to think you are. Now, I'd like to ask a favor I'm not entitled to. I did my duty as I saw it, and gave you my advice as an officer of the S.D. Now I'm asking for a privilege as an old friend. If you're going to try bringing that ship in, I'd like to be aboard her on the way. I want to be there when they come to. I'm a qualified observer and it shouldn't take more than an hour to get me up there. It won't be much of a delay."

The Commander's voice was icy. "I think you know that's impossible, Bob. Certainly you're qualified—too qualified. We have to have a man on that ship, but we only need one man, and he has to be expendable. The only qualifications he needs are to know how to pilot the ship, and to be able to talk continuously. We already have a volunteer for the job, and he's acceptable. If you want to give him any instructions about what to look for or what to talk about, you have five minutes to prepare them. After that, the action will start. You understand, I am taking your advice. But I feel I must first prove to myself that your premises are correct. I want to see just how irresistible they are."

He turned to the P.R. Chief, and went on as coldly: "You are free to leave now, Miss Ardin. You'll want to hear the reports as they come in, I imagine. It should be about twenty minutes before the ship is actually under way."

Pfc. Joe Fromm walked through the inner airlock into the BB-3, climbed out of his space suit, and made a quick examination of the cabins. Three of the aliens, still unconscious, were bound ankle to ankle and wrist to wrist on the floor of one cabin. That door was to be locked. The other cabin was empty, as it was supposed to be.

"Cabins okay as planned," he muttered into the mouthpiece, strapped to his chest. "Corridor and cabinets clear." He entered the control room, and tested the manacles restraining the outside limbs of the alien who had formerly occupied the pilot's seat, and was now secured in a specially built chair. "Alien in control room unconscious and I'd say pretty safe, the way he's tied down. Instrument check: electronic controls, okay; radar, okay; rocket controls . . ."

He went down the list, cheerful with the familiar routine, talking easily, untroubled by the need for extra breaths between words that had plagued his inspection of the aliens.

"I am now strapping myself into the pilot-seat, and preparing for takeoff. Ready to leave as soon as I am signaled free . . . signal received, blasting off now . . . utilizing minimum acceleration, coming in at Deimos on direct approach . . . the fella in the control room here seems to be wiggling his toes . . . you wouldn't think they'd have toes just like us, would you? . . . he's coming to, all right . . . I am on direct course to Deimos at min-axe still . . . I think maybe everything'll work out okay . . ."

He had to watch the instruments with one eye and the alien with the other. The—whatever he was—didn't seem to be trying to bust loose at all.

"He's moving his head now, and looking around . . . looking at his handcuffs, and the chair, trying to turn his head around to see where his legs are cuffed underneath, but he isn't struggling at all . . . looking me over now . . . I caught his eye for a minute just then, or he caught mine. I think he wants me to look at him again, but I'll try not to. He has to be able to fasten my attention on something to hypnotize me, doesn't he? I am moving my eyes around, checking instruments, and thinking as many different thoughts as I can. . . .

"We are now approaching an orbit around Mars, decelerating. My radar screen shows two Scanliters following us . . . should they be so close inside range in case it is necessary to fire on us? . . . Please don't . . . *that's not my thought!*

"It . . . he's thinking at me . . . they are telepaths, all right. He doesn't seem to, I don't know, the first thought I was sure wasn't mine was, please don't fire on us, we are friends. It seemed so natural I started to say it. His thoughts aren't in clear words now. . . . I heard once that to 'receive' stuff like this you have to not concentrate . . . something like that. Maybe I'm trying too hard . . . No. *I'm too tense* . . . that was *his* thought, not mine, he was telling me not to be so tense and I'd understand. . . .

"He says—you can call it 'says'; it's enough like talking —he says they're friends, they like us. They want to be friends. He keeps saying it different ways but it's the same feeling all the time, with different—pictures, I guess to go with it. . . ."

Pictures! Hey, stay out of there!

"He wants me to . . . to *love* him. That's what he says. He . . . *men don't feel that way about each other* . . . *no!* . . . loves me, he loves all—not men, some kind of thought for his own people, and all—living creatures —those are on his home planet. He loves all men, this time he means men."

That was silly of me . . . he wasn't being nasty . . . he just meant love . . . that picture was mine . . .

"He says the pictures I get for meanings are all my own, so I might get his meaning wrong sometimes. He makes a picture in his mind, the way he'd visualize a thought on his world, but I see it the way it would be on mine. . . .

"Listen, Captain Malcolm just didn't understand. This *is* important . . . they don't mean the kind of thing we do when they say 'love.' They mean liking and sharing and . . . we haven't got the right words for it, but it's all

right. It's not a grabby feeling, or taking anything, or
hurting anybody. There's nothing to be afraid of. The
only thing that Captain got right was that story about
the kid. . . ."

On Phobos Base, Lucy Ardin's typer clacked eagerly,
while Bill Hartson and Bob Schwartz turned from the
viewer together. Hartson was a soldier; his face was stern
and set, as he reached for the mike. The only emotion
he showed was the single flash from his eyes to his
friend's when he looked at Schwartz and saw the tears of
frustration rolling unashamed down the psychofficer's
face.

". . . the one who threw the note over the wall. That is
the way they feel. He's telling me now, to tell all of you,
he's agreeing, he says I understand now, it's the way
human beings love when they're kids, like the note the
girl wrote: Whoever you are . . ."

The Commander spoke one word. "Apple."

". . . I love you."

CONNECTION
COMPLETED

HELLO, DARLING.
I'm glad you waited.
I couldn't do anything else. She smiled wryly. *I'm glad I waited, too. Hello.*

He saw her through the window, sitting alone in a pool of white light, on a white chair, at a white table, almost exactly centered in the expanse of white-tiled floor. She was wearing the green suit and the gray-green scarf with the narrow border of pink rose on it. Her back was toward him, but he knew beyond doubt it was she: her hair, over the scarf, was the same dark mist that floated in his mind, cool and caressing, tickling the filaments of his imagination.

He stood out there on the sidewalk in the chill city drizzle, staring in through the plate glass window of the cafeteria, waiting for her to make some move, any move that would confirm or deny: to turn around and show her face, looking as he knew it must; or to vanish as suddenly and completely as the elusive fantasy he also knew she had to be. He stood there waiting, mostly, for his own shock to give way to decision. *Go in? Go away?*

"Move along, Mac!"

Todd jerked his head around, eyes wide and startled, then narrowing in anger at the dough-faced cop.

"Is that a new law?" he sneered. "Something wrong with standing on the street?"

"Not so you just stand there," the policeman said. Then,

in a different tone: "Sorry, doc. It was just the way you was looking in the window."

"You mean hungry?" Todd didn't feel like being reasonable. The apology was to his clothes anyhow; not to him. "Well, I am. You know any better reason to look in a restaurant?" If the cop got mad enough, there wouldn't be any impossible decision to make; he'd be in night court, paying a fine instead.

The cop didn't get mad. He shook his head tiredly and wandered off; muttering. Todd turned back to the window, and the girl had moved.

She was getting up. She had her check in her hand, and she was reaching for her raincoat on the next chair. Immediately, urgently, Todd wanted her not to go.

Sit still, he begged. You waited this long, don't spoil it now. I'm coming, kid. I shouldn't have stalled like that, but I'm coming in now. Just wait a minute.

He was walking fast up the block toward the door, watching her through the window all the time, and he saw her change her mind and settle back in the chair again. She never turned around. He still hadn't seen her face.

He pushed through the door into warm dry air, struggling with the corners of his mouth, keeping his smile underneath his skin. He couldn't very well walk in on her with a triumphant smirk all over his face. There was no reason to assume that she *knew*.

She didn't; he was sure of that when he saw the baffled defeat in the set of her shoulders as she leaned back in her chair and picked up the coffee cup again. The cup was empty; he knew that. She realized it a moment later, and set it down again, and looked up straight ahead of her at the big clock on the wall.

What on earth am I sitting here for? She made a restless, irritable motion toward her raincoat.

Hey, wait a minute! he pleaded. *Don't go now. Just give me time to think of something.*

What did she expect? To have him walk over and say "Pardon me, but aren't you the girl in my dreams?"

She didn't expect anything. She didn't even know who he was. But she turned and looked out the window while he crossed the big room to the counter at the back. *It's still raining,* she satisfied herself. *I might as well sit here.* She picked up a folded newspaper, and Todd stared across the perforated metal drip-board of the counter, into a dry, yellow-wrinkled face.

"Coffee—black," he said, and waited while brown liquid flushed slowly out of the urn into a thick tan mug. He tried to find her image in the mirror on the sidewall, but the angle was distorting; all he could tell was that she was still there, waiting.

For what?

He wasn't even sure who asked the question, let alone whether it had an answer. He couldn't trust the certainty he felt. He hadn't even seen her face yet.

The dry wrinkled face pushed a mug at him across the counter.

"Sugarncream?"

Todd shook his head. "No, thanks." He fumbled in his pocket for change, cursing his clumsy fingers, suddenly sure she would be gone when he turned around. Then:

Didn't I say "black" before? he wondered. He had to watch out. Ever since this thing started, he had been worried about things like that. How could you tell if you were just going off your rocker? How could you know whether you remembered to say things out loud at all?

You did. I heard you.

That's a big help! You heard me! I can hear you too, he snapped at her, *and you never said a word out loud! Hell, I don't know if you even thought a word!*

He could just as easily be talking to himself. He was, anyhow. Even if this was all real, actually happening—even if he wasn't just tripping a light fantastic down the path to a padded cell—he was still just talking to himself, effectively, until he was sure that she *knew.*

Stop fighting it, man! It's real, all right.

He had the dime in his hand finally, flung it across the counter, picked up his mug, slopping coffee over the sides, and headed toward her table, with the familiar feeling of her smile lingering in his head after the words began to fade.

The place was almost empty. There was no excuse for sitting at her table—except the obvious one, that he had come in for just that purpose. He sat down directly across from her, took one quick look at her face, and it was all wrong. It wasn't the face that went with the green suit. She wasn't smiling. And she didn't seem to be aware that he was there.

Todd burned his tongue on his coffee, and took another look over the edge of the cup. This time he caught her by surprise and she turned away swiftly when their glances met. She was aware of him, then; and she was frightened!

Scared stiff! she assured him. *You're not real. I don't believe in you. Get out of here, will you? God damn it, get out!*

The vehemence of it almost convinced him. He wouldn't be shrieking at himself that way—or would he? What did he know about how a person feels inside when he's slipping his gears? It made sense for her to feel just as scared and mad inside as he did . . . but if the whole thing was originating inside his own mind, it made even more sense for her to sound that way. . . .

He knew just where that train of thought went: round and round and all the way back round again. He put down his coffee cup, made a face over it, and looked straight at her.

"Would you pass the sugar please?" he said, and waited, watching.

She was scared, all right. Scared, or very tired, or both. He noticed, now, that there were long deep lines running down from the inside corners of her eyes, along her nose, outlining tight-bunched muscles; another set of lines striking down from the edges of her mouth; a taut set of defiance to her jaw. And in the same instant, he realized her eyes were gray-green like the scarf, as he knew they ought to be, and her lipstick was soft coral-pink like the roses on the scarf.

She was reaching for the jar of sugar automatically. Her face showed no reaction, no memory of what he *thought* had happened a few minutes earlier, at the counter. He tried transposing her features, in his mind, setting them in the other expression, the only one he'd "seen" before, relaxing all the tense muscles, turning up the lips into a smile of warm acceptance. . . .

"Here," she said impatiently, holding the jar under his nose. He looked from her face to her hand and back again, wondering how long she'd been holding it there while he stared at her. If she was the wrong girl—*if there was no right girl*—

There was a very small smile on her face now. Nothing like the look he was used to, but enough so he was certain it was the same face.

Well, do you want it or don't you?

She meant the sugar, he realized after an instant's pause. "Thanks. I don't usually use it," he started to explain, and watched the same struggle on her face that he remembered feeling on his own as he walked into the place: the effort to suppress apparently unwarranted laughter.

He let the explanation drift off, and realized he'd done what he'd been worried about all this time: answered aloud what he had heard only inside his ears.

In that case, she could be laughing at him just because of his confusion and insanity. She could . . . she could be anything or anyone, but she also *could be* the girl who had haunted his waking and sleeping dreams for the last six months.

"Thanks," he said again, and relieved her of the sugar jar.

You better think of something better than that. I can't keep sitting here much longer. "You're welcome," she said. *I . . . imagined . . . I thought about you as a sort of fluent character. Not the tongue-tied kind . . .*

I don't usually have so much trouble. You're not yourself exactly, either . . .

"Pardon me, miss," he asked courteously, "I wonder if you happen to know whether there's a post office open anywhere near here? At this hour, I mean?" *Pretty feeble, I know, babe, but you're rushing me. . . .*

"I don't think . . . there's one that *might* be open, but

I'm not sure. It's just about five blocks. You turn to the left at the corner, and . . ."

He didn't listen to the rest. He didn't need a post office for anything.

Oh, my God! her voice screamed inside his head. What am I doing now? I've never seen this man before. I don't, I don't, I don't, know who he is or anything about him! He looks like . . . he looks like somebody I invented, but that's an accident, it has to be! Daydreaming isn't so bad . . . anybody who's lonely daydreams . . . but when you start having hallucinations . . .

Yeah, I know! It's time to go look up a good reliable old-fashioned psychiatrist and tell him all your troubles. Don't think you're the only one, babe.

He watched her eyes flick to the phone booth in the corner, and realized he'd meant in the directory when he thought the words "look up."

There was a way to find out after all!

"I suppose I could call from here and find out if they're open," he said. *Calm yourself, fellow, he told himself. You could have thought about the directory after she looked that way. It's hard to be sure about subjective time-sequence.*

The thing to do was set it up ahead of time, make sure she knew what he was doing—or as sure as he could be— and then see what happened.

"That's a good idea," she said flatly . . . and began making motions at her handbag and raincoat again. It took swering, of course, his remark about calling the post swering, of course, his remark about calling the post office.

"Nasty weather," he said brightly. "Hate to go wandering around out there for nothing." *Please darling . . . stick it out a little longer . . . I know I'm being dumb, but I don't know much about picking up a girl.*

Well, I don't usually get picked up!

"Would you care for some more coffee?" he said desperately, rising before she had a chance to get her things together. "Could I bring it back?" *Listen, listen good, now . . . if you want to try a test of this thing, listen good . . .*

She hesitated, holding the bag in her hand, her arm half-extended toward the next chair where her raincoat was draped over the back of the seat.

Now, listen: if you want to try a test, just to find out, let me know by putting your bag in your other hand, and then putting it down on the table . . .

He watched anxiously.

"Well-l-l . . . thank you." She smiled tightly, and transferred her bag from her right hand to the left, then set it down, carefully, as though jarring might explode it, on the left-hand side of her empty cup.

Todd heard himself saying smoothly, naturally, "Do you take cream and sugar?" It was startling that his voice should behave so well, when every nerve cell and fiber in him was vibrating with incredulous exaltation. He wanted to reach out and grab her, hold her face between his two hands, pull her head to rest on his shoulder, soothe her, explain, reassure, until the sharp-etched lines of fear and tension vanished from her face and he could see her, *really her*, not in a dream or vision or in some unknown receptive part of his mind, but see her in the flesh, smiling with her whole face as she always had before.

And he couldn't do it.

Not yet.

He'd planned that first request to be a signal, nothing more. It wasn't enough to go on. It could be coincidence, accident; he might even have anticipated from some unconscious memory of an earlier action of hers, that that move was the one she would make, and so have set up the signal to get the answer he wanted.

This time it wouldn't be like that.

"I'll make that phone call, and bring the coffee back with me," he told her slowly and distinctly. She nodded, and then he thought as clearly as he could:

Only if you hear me, baby, if you understand and want to believe it like I do, don't wait for me to bring it back. You get the coffees while I'm in the booth. You understand? Do you, babe? You get the coffees while I go in the phone booth . . . then I'll know for sure. You wouldn't do that for any other reason, see? That way I'll know. You just do that, and you can leave the rest to me . . . Understand?

She was nodding again. *All right. Go ahead. I understand.* But there was a feeling of irritation—or impatience? He couldn't tell. *Go on. Hurry up.*

Impatience. He turned and walked across the white-tiled floor, his heels sounding loud and hollow all the way. He didn't look around. He was sure she understood. He knew she was somehow irritated. He didn't know what she would do. But what he had to do was walk across the endless rows of tiles to the phone booth, and not give himself any chance to give her a signal of any kind—in case he was wrong.

He didn't trust himself to give her enough time if he faked it, so he looked up the post office in the directory, and stepped into the booth, pulled the door shut, without ever looking around, put his coin into the slot, and let the number ring twenty times before he hung up again and stepped out.

He glanced at the counter, and the wrinkle-faced man was leaning back against the wall next to the coffee urn, turning a racing form over in his hand. He looked toward the table, then, and she was gone.

Handbag, raincoat, green suit, scarf, and all. Gone.

You little fool!

The thought was hopeless and tender and the loneliest thought of his life. He was at the door, looking out, up and down the street but she was gone completely, vanished, like . . .

Like the illusion she was?

He went back to the table, or tried to. He couldn't find it. He wanted to see her coffee cup there; he thought she might have left the newspaper she was reading. Something, anything, to prove she had been there, flesh and blood, a real girl. Not just an image his own mind had made for him six months ago, to live with and talk to—and love.

Nothing. All the tables in the center of the room were

clear and clean. There was a boy dumping cups and clattering silver in the far corner. Todd strode over, stood behind him, and couldn't think what to say.

"Did you take two cups off a table over there?" It sounded ridiculous.

The boy looked around, sleepy, stupid, glazed-eyed. "Huh?"

I said, "Did you take some coffee cups off a table just now?"

"Sure, doc. That's what they pay me for."

Todd shook his head impatiently, like clicking a telephone receiver, trying to clear the line. "Look," he said slowly. "Right about the middle of the room there's a table I was sitting at. Then I went to the phone booth. When I came back, the dishes were gone. Did you just clear that table off?"

"Listen, Mister, if you wasn't done with your coffee, you shouldn't of left it there. All I know is, a table is empty, I clear it off. How should I know . . ."

"I was done." He made himself relax outwardly, realizing that his stance, his voice, his eyes were all threatening the youngster. "It's all right. I was finished. All I want to know is, were there . . . did you take a newspaper off of there?"

"A paper?" The boy looked doubtfully at the bottom rack of his pushwagon. "Lessee now . . . there was a paper on one of them tables. . . ." He reached and brought forth a folded sheet. Todd gazed at it helplessly. He hadn't noticed which paper she was reading. He couldn't tell if that was the one.

"Did you . . . was that on a table with two coffee cups?"

"Gee, mister, I don't know. . . ." The boy was really trying to remember, Todd realized, with surprise. Trying hard. "Yeah I guess . . . listen, mister, if it's so important I won't kid you. I don't know, that's all see?"

"Okay kid. Thanks. Thanks a lot." Todd fished a coin out of his pocket, pushed it into the startled boy's hand, and turned and walked out. Where to, he didn't know; but he had to get out of there. The girl wasn't coming back, that much he was sure of. That is, if there was a girl. If ever there had been a girl with a green suit and a mist of dark hair, and a face that smiled for him in memory.

It was cold and wet outside, and that suited him fine. He paced the sidewalk, out of lamplight into shadow, and back into damp reflections of the light. Mica particles in the gray cement flashed like tiny distant stars or signaling fireflies under his eyes. Unseen drops of moisture chilled the back of his neck, damped the edge of his collar. He stepped off the curb, and a car screeched, braking, around the corner avoiding him by inches.

All these things he perceived, but without meaning. Perception was suddenly a frightening thing, to be examined and tested every time before you could trust it. What you saw was not necessarily there at all. What you wanted, you could not see, or else you saw without reality. He felt the cold rain on his skin, but put no faith in it, because it was all a part of the girl and the night and the illusion he had made for himself.

He turned a corner, walking faster. No sense trying to avoid obstacles, or dodge moving objects, if you didn't know for sure that they were there. He crossed another street, and walked faster still. He didn't know where he was going, and if he knew it wouldn't matter, because when he got to the end of the journey, he still wouldn't know where he was.

The city flashed its distractions. Sights and sounds and odors, moisture, temperature, touch assailed him, and could not penetrate his isolation.

A man lives all his life inside the wall of his own skull, making words into sentences, moving muscles to form gestures, so that he can make his existence and purposes known to others; and in the same way, absorbing his perceptions of the people and things around him, trying to interpret as best he can, so as to understand some part of their meaning for himself. But he never gets outside the bony barriers of his own head, or past the hardening defenses of others. For every human being, the word or the gesture has some slightly different meaning.

No two people ever meet completely without some slight or great distortion of intent or understanding, occurring in the jangled complexity of living cells that make up the expressive and interpretive mechanisms of the man.

Todd Harmacher made this discovery, as most men do, when he was very small. Each contact of the thirty-odd years since had served to confirm it. Each contact until, for a few brief minutes this evening, he had let himself believe that he was truly, entirely, in communication with another human being, rather than with some strangely shaped and ill-portented section of his own imagination.

Now he paced the city streets, oblivious to rain and cold, defying noise and light, aware of the potentialities of total loneliness as he had never quite envisioned it before.

He crossed another street and turned a corner, for no reason except the inner urgency that said, *Turn! Here! Now!*

Stop!

He stopped.

Perception invaded him. He was standing in front of an old stone building, a relic of the city's first pride in size and strength, gray and massive and dirty. A lamppost down the street threw a flood of light along the rain-soaked sidewalk, but the doorway directly in front of him was dark. And her smiling face was in his head again, framed by the soft scarf, the drifting mist of her hair touching gently against the bitterness and anger in his mind.

I'm sorry, dear, she told him, but I got so scared! I used to think I made you up, then for a while I thought you were real. Then I told myself that was nonsense, and I learned to live with a dream. . . .

I know. I know!

And then when I saw you, I got frightened. And when I started doing things I didn't mean to do. . . .

Poor darling! I shouldn't have . . .

No! Don't you see? That's when I knew it was real!

But then . . .?

But then I knew you still didn't believe it yourself, and I thought, if I did as you asked each time, you'd never

never know which one of us it was, or whether I was really here. So . . . so when you weren't looking, I ran out, and came here and called you and waited. . . .

He couldn't see her in the darkness of the doorway, but he knew. They both knew now. He knew, too, what her face would look like if he could see it at this moment, but, knowing, he didn't have to see it.

"Hi, babe," he said, stepping forward gladly into the dark doorway. "I'm glad you waited."

"I couldn't do anything else," she said wryly. Then he opened his arms to her, and she said, "I'm glad I waited, too. Hello."

DEAD
CENTER

THEY GAVE
him sweet ices, and kissed him all round, and the
Important People who had come to dinner all smiled in
a special way as his mother took him from the living
room and led him down the hall to his own bedroom.

"Great kid you got there," they said to Jock, his father,
and "Serious little bugger, isn't he?" Jock didn't say anything, but Toby knew he would be grinning, looking
pleased and embarrassed. Then their voices changed, and
that meant they had begun to talk about the important
events for which the important people had come.

In his own room, Toby wriggled his toes between crisp
sheets, and breathed in the powder-and-perfume smell
of his mother as she bent over him for a last hurried
goodnight kiss. There was no use asking for a story tonight. Toby lay still and waited while she closed the door
behind her and went off to the party, click-tap, tip-clack,
hurrying on her high silver heels. She had heard the voices
change back there too, and she didn't want to miss anything. Toby got up and opened his door just a crack, and
set himself down in back of it, and listened.

In the big square living room, against the abstract patterns of gray and vermilion and chartreuse, the men and
women moved in easy patterns of familiar acts. Coffee,
brandy, cigarette, cigar. Find your partner, choose your
seat. Jock sprawled with perfect relaxed contentment on
the low couch with the deep red corduroy cover. Tim
O'Heyer balanced nervously on the edge of the same
couch, wreathed in cigar-smoke, small and dark and alert.
Gordon Kimberly dwarfed the big easy chair with the
bulking importance of him. Ben Stein, shaggy and rumpled

as ever, was running a hand through his hair till it too stood on end. He was leaning against a window frame, one hand on the back of the straight chair in which his wife Sue sat, erect and neat and proper and chic, dressed in smart black that set off perfectly her precise blonde beauty. Mrs. Kimberly, just enough overstuffed so that her pearls gave the appearance of actually choking her, was the only stranger to the house. She was standing near the doorway, politely admiring Toby's personal art gallery, as Allie Madero valiantly strove to explain each minor masterpiece.

Ruth Kruger stood still a moment, surveying her room and her guests. Eight of them, herself included, and all Very Important People. In the familiar comfort of her own living room, the idea made her giggle. Allie and Mrs. Kimberly both turned to her, questioning. She laughed and shrugged, helpless to explain, and they all went across the room to join the others.

"Guts," O'Heyer said through the cloud of smoke. "How do you do it, Jock? Walk out of a setup like this into . . . God knows what?"

"Luck," Jock corrected him. "A setup like this helps. I'm the world's pampered darling and I know it."

"Faith is what he means," Ben put in. "He just gets by believing that last year's luck is going to hold up. So it does."

"Depends on what you mean by luck. If you think of it as a vector sum composed of predictive powers and personal ability and accurate information and . . ."

"Charm and nerve and . . ."

"Guts," Tim said again, interrupting the interrupter.

"All right, all of them," Ben agreed. "Luck is as good a word as any to cover the combination."

"We're all lucky people." That was Allie, drifting into range, with Ruth behind him. "We just happened to get born at the right time with the right dream. Any one of us, fifty years ago, would have been called a wild-eyed visiona—"

"Any one of us," Kimberly said heavily, "fifty ago,

would have had a different dream—in time with the times."

Jock smiled, and let them talk, not joining in much. He listened to philosophy and compliments and speculations and comments, and lay sprawled across the comfortable couch in his own living rom, with his wife's hand under his own, consciously letting his mind play back and forth between the two lives he lived: this, here . . . and the perfect mathematic bleakness of the metal beast that would be his home in three days' time.

He squeezed his wife's hand, and she turned and looked at him, and there was no doubt a man could have about what the world held in store.

When they had all gone, Jock walked down the hall and picked up the little boy asleep on the floor, and put him back into his bed. Toby woke up long enough to grab his father's hand and ask earnestly, out of the point in the conversation where sleep had overcome him:

"Daddy, if the universe hasn't got any ends to it, how can you tell where you are?"

"Me?" Jock asked. "I'm right next to the middle of it."

"How do you *know*?"

His father tapped him lightly on the chest.

"Because that's where the middle is." Jock smiled and stood up. "Go to sleep, champ. Good night."

And Toby slept, while the universe revolved in all its mystery about the small center Jock Kruger had assigned to it.

"Scared?" she asked, much later, in the spaceless silence of their bedroom.

He had to think about it before he could answer. "I guess not. I guess I think I ought to be, but I'm not. I don't think I'd do it at all if I wasn't sure." He was almost asleep, when the thought hit him, and he jerked awake and saw she was sure enough lying wide-eyed and sleepless beside him. "*Baby!*" he said, and it was almost an accusation. "Baby, you're not scared, are you?"

"Not if you're not," she said. But they never could lie to each other.

II

Toby sat on the platform, next to his grandmother. They were in the second row, right in back of his mother and father, so it was all right for him to wriggle a little bit, or whisper. They couldn't hear much of the speeches back there, and what they did hear mostly didn't make sense to Toby. But every now and then Grandma would grab his hand tight all of a sudden, and he understood what the whole thing was about: it was because Daddy was going away again.

His Grandma's hand was very white, with little red and tan dots in it, and big blue veins that stood out higher than the wrinkles in her skin, whenever she grabbed at his hand. Later, walking over to the towering skyscraping rocket, he held his mother's hand; it was smooth and cool and tan, all one color, and she didn't grasp at him the way Grandma did. Later still, his father's two hands, picking him up to kiss, were bigger and darker tan than his mother's, not so smooth, and the fingers were stronger, but so strong it hurt sometimes.

They took him up in an elevator, and showed him all around the inside of the rocket, where Daddy would sit, and where all the food was stored, for emergency, they said, and the radio and everything. Then it was time to say goodbye.

Daddy was laughing at first, and Toby tried to laugh, too, but he didn't really want Daddy to go away. Daddy kissed him, and he felt like crying because it was scratchy against Daddy's cheek, and the strong fingers were hurting him now. Then Daddy stopped laughing and looked at him very seriously. "You take care of your mother, now," Daddy told him. "You're a big boy this time."

"Okay," Toby said. Last time Daddy went away in a rocket, he was not-quite-four, and they teased him with the peom in the book that said, *James James Morrison Morrison Weatherby George Dupree, Took great care of his mother, though he was only three.* . . . So Toby didn't much like Daddy saying that now, because he knew they didn't really mean it.

"Okay," he said, and then because he was angry, he said, "Only she's supposed to take care of me, isn't she?"

Daddy and Mommy both laughed, and so did the two men who were standing there waiting for Daddy to get done saying goodbye to him. He wriggled, and Daddy put him down.

"I'll bring you a piece of the moon, son," Daddy said, and Toby said, "All right, fine." He reached for his mother's hand, but he found himself hanging onto Grandma instead, because Mommy and Daddy were kissing each other, and both of them had forgotten all about him.

He thought they were never going to get done kissing.

Ruth Kruger stood in the glass control booth with her son on one side of her, and Gordon Kimberly breathing heavily on the other side. *Something's wrong,* she thought, *this time something's wrong.* And then, swiftly, *I mustn't think that way!*

Jealous? she taunted herself. *Do you want* something to be wrong, just because this one isn't all yours, because Argent did some of it?

But if anything is wrong, she prayed, let it be now, right away, so he can't go. If anything's wrong let it be in the firing gear or the . . . what? Even now, it was too late. The beast was too big and too delicate and too precise. If something went wrong, even now, it was too late. It was . . .

You didn't finish that thought. Not if you were Ruth Kruger, and your husband was Jock Kruger, and nobody knew but the two of you how much of the courage that had gone twice round the moon, and was about to land on it, was yours. When a man knows his wife's faith is unshakeable, he can't help coming back. (But: "Baby! You're not scared, are you?")

Twice around the moon, and they called him Jumping Jock. There was never a doubt in anyone's mind who'd pilot the KIM-5, the bulky beautiful beast out there today. Kruger and Kimberly, O'Heyer and Stein. It was a combo.

It won every time. *Every time.* Nothing to doubt. No room for doubt.

"Minus five . . ." someone said into a mike, and there was perfect quiet all around. "Four . . . three . . .

(But he held me too tight, and he laughed too loud. . . .)

(Only because he thought *I* was scared, she answered herself.)

". . . Mar—"

You didn't even hear the whole word, because the thunder-drumming roar of the beast itself split your ears.

Ringing quiet came down and she caught up Toby, held him tight, tight. . . .

"Perfect!" Gordon Kimberly sighed. "*Perfect!*"

So if anything was wrong, it hadn't showed up yet.

She put Toby down, then took his hand. "Come on," she said. "I'll buy you an ice-cream soda." He grinned at her. He'd been looking very strange all day, but now he looked real again. His hair had got messed up when she grabbed him.

"We're having cocktails for the press in the conference room," Kimberly said. "I think we could find something Toby would like."

"Wel-l-l-l . . ." She didn't want a cocktail, and she didn't want to talk to the press. "I think maybe we'll beg off this time. . . ."

"I think there might be some disappointment—" the man started; then Tim O'Heyer came dashing up.

"Come on, babe," he said. "Your old man told me to take personal charge while he was gone." He leered. On him it looked cute. She laughed. Then she looked down at Toby. "What would you rather, Tobe? Want to go out by ourselves, or go to the party?"

"I don't care," he said.

Tim took the boy's hand. "What we were thinking of was having a kind of party here, and then I think they're going to bring some dinner in, and anybody who wants to can stay up till your Daddy gets to the moon. That'll be pretty late. I guess you wouldn't want to stay up late like that, would you?"

Somebody else talking to Toby like that would be all wrong, but Tim was a friend, Toby's friend too. Ruth still didn't want to go to the party, but she remembered now that there had been plans for something like that all along, and since Toby was beginning to look eager, and it was important to keep the press on their side . . .

"You win, O'Heyer," she said. "Will somebody please send out for an ice-cream soda? Cherry syrup, I think it is this week . . ." She looked inquiringly at her son. ". . . and . . . strawberry ice cream?"

Tim shuddered. Toby nodded. Ruth smiled, and they all went in to the party.

"Well, young man!" Toby thought the redheaded man in the brown suit was probably what they called a reporter, but he wasn't sure. "How about it? You going along next time?"

"I don't know," Toby said politely. "I guess not."

"Don't you want to be a famous flier like your Daddy?" a strange woman in an evening gown asked him.

"I don't know," he muttered, and looked around for his mother, but he couldn't see her.

They kept asking him questions like that, about whether he wanted to go to the moon. Daddy said he was too little. You'd think all these people would know that much.

Jock Kruger came up swiftly out of dizzying darkness into isolation and clarity. As soon as he could move his head, before he fully remembered why, he began checking the dials and meters and flashing lights on the banked panel in front of him. He was fully aware of the ship, of its needs and strains and motion, before he came to complete consciousness of himself, his weightless body, his purpose, or his memories.

But he was aware of himself as a part of the ship before he remembered his name, so that by the time he knew he had a face and hands and innards, these parts were already occupied with feeding the beast's human brain a carefully prepared stimulant out of a nippled flask fastened in front of his head.

He pressed a button under his index finger in the arm rest of the couch that held him strapped to safety.

"Hi," he said. "Is anybody up besides me?"

He pressed the button under his middle finger and waited.

Not for long.

"Thank God!" a voice crackled out of the loudspeaker. "You really conked out this time, Jock. Nothing wrong?"

"Not so I'd know it. You want . . . How long was I out?"

"Twenty-three minutes, eighteen seconds, takeoff to reception. Yeah. Give us a log reading."

Methodically, in order, he read off the pointers and numbers on the control panel, the colors and codes and swinging needles and quiet ones that told him how each muscle and nerve and vital organ of the great beast was taking the trip. He did it slowly and with total concentration. Then, when he was all done, there was nothing else to do except sit back and start wondering about that big blackout.

It shouldn't have happened. It never happened before. There was nothing in the compendium of information he'd just sent back to Earth to account for it.

A different ship, different . . . different men. Two and a half years different. Years of easy living and . . . growing old? Too old for this game?

Twenty-three minutes!

Last time it was under ten The first time maybe 90 seconds more. It didn't matter, of course, not at takeoff. There was nothing for him to do then. Nothing now. Nothing for four more hours. He was there to put the beast back down on . . .

He grinned, and felt like Jock Kruger again. Identity returned complete. This time he was there to put the beast down where no man or beast had ever been before. This time they were going to the moon.

III

Ruth Kruger sipped at a cocktail and murmured responses to the admiring, the curious, the envious, the hopeful, and the hate-full ones who spoke to her. She was waiting for something, and after an unmeasurable stretch of time Allie Madero brought it to her.

First a big smile seeking her out across the room, so she knew it had come. Then a low-voiced confirmation.

"Wasn't it . . . an awful long time?" she asked. She hadn't been watching the clock, on purpose, but she was sure it was longer than it should have been.

Allie stopped smiling. "Twenty-three," she said.

Ruth gasped. "What . . . ?"

"You figure it. I can't."

"There's nothing in the ship. I mean nothing was changed that would account for it." She shook her head slowly. This time she didn't know the ship well enough to talk like that. There could be something. Oh, *Jock!* "I don't know," she said. "Too many people worked on that thing. I . . ."

"Mrs. Kruger!" It was the redheaded reporter, the obnoxious one. "We just got the report on the blackout. I'd like a statement from you, if you don't mind, as designer of the ship—"

"I am not the designer of this ship," she said coldly.

"You worked on the design, didn't you?"

"Yes."

"Well, then, to the best of your knowledge . . . ?"

"To the best of my knowledge, there is no change in design to account for Mr. Kruger's prolonged unconsciousness. Had there been any such prognosis, the press would have been informed."

"Mrs. Kruger, I'd like to ask you whether you feel that the innovations made by Mr. Argent could—"

"Aw, lay off, will you?" Allie broke in, trying to be casual and kidding about it; but behind her own flaming cheeks, Ruth was aware of her friend's matching anger. "How much do you want to milk this for, anyhow? So the guy conked out an extra ten minutes. If you want somebody to crucify for it, why don't you pick on one of us who doesn't happen to be married to him?" She turned to Ruth before the man could answer. "Where's

Toby? He's probably about ready to bust from cookies and carbonation."

"He's in the lounge," the reporter put in. "Or he was a few minutes—"

Ruth and Allie started off without waiting for the rest. The redhead had been talking to the kid. No telling how many of them were on top of him now.

"I thought Tim was with him," Ruth said hastily, then she thought of something, and turned back long enough to say: "For the record, Mr. . . . uh . . . I know of no criticism that can be made of any of the work done by Mr. Argent." Then she went to find her son.

There was nothing to do and nothing to see except the instrument meters and dials to check and log and check and log again. Radio stations all around Earth were beamed on him. He could have kibitzed his way to the moon, but he didn't want to. He was thinking.

Thinking back, and forward, and right in this moment. Thinking of the instant's stiffness of Ruth's body when she said she wasn't scared, and the rambling big house on the hill, and Toby politely agreeing when he offered to bring him back a piece of the moon.

Thinking of Toby's growing up some day, and how little he really knew about his son, and what would they do, Toby and Ruth, if anything . . .

He'd never thought that way before. He'd never thought anything except to know he'd come back, because he couldn't stay away. It was always that simple. He couldn't stay away now, either. That hadn't changed. But as he sat there, silent and useless for the time, it occurred to him that he'd left something out of his calculations. Luck, they'd been talking about. Yes, he'd had luck. But—what was it Sue had said about a vector sum?— there was more to figure in than your own reflexes and the beast's strength. There was the *outside*. Space . . . environment . . . God . . . destiny. What difference does it make what name you give it?

He couldn't stay away . . . but maybe he could be *kept* away.

He'd never thought that way before.

"You tired, honey?"

"No," he said. "I'm just sick of this party. I want to go home."

"It'll be over pretty soon, Toby. I think as long as we stayed this long we better wait for . . . for the end of the party."

"It's a silly party. You said you'd buy me an ice-cream soda."

"I did, darling," she said patiently. "At least, if I didn't buy it, I got it for you. You had it, didn't you?"

"Yes but you *said* we'd go *out* and have one."

"Look. Why don't you just put your head down on my lap and . . ."

"I'm no *baby!* Anyhow I'm not tired."

"All right. We'll go pretty soon. You just sit here on the couch, and you don't have to talk to anybody if you don't feel like it. I'll tell you what. I'll go find you a magazine or a book or something to look at, and—"

"I don't *want* a magazine. I want my own book with the pirates in it."

"You just stay put a minute, so I can find you. I'll bring you something."

She got up and went out to the other part of the building where the officers were, and collected an assortment of leaflets and folders with shiny bright pictures of mail rockets and freight transports and jets and visionary moon rocket designs, and took them back to the little lounge where she'd left him.

She looked at the clock on the way. Twenty-seven more minutes. There was *no* reason to believe that anything was wrong.

They were falling now. A man's body is not equipped to sense direction *toward* or *from*, up or down, without the help of landmarks or gravity. But the body of the beast was designed to know such things; and Kruger, at the nerve center, knew everything the beast knew.

Ship is extension of self, and self is—extension or limitation?—of ship. If Jock Kruger is the center of the universe—remember the late night after the party, and picking Toby off the floor?—then ship is extension of self, and the man is the brain of the beast. But if ship is universe—certainly continuum; that's universe, isn't it?— then the weakling man-thing in the couch is a limiting condition of the universe. A human brake. He was there to make it stop where it didn't "want" to.

Suppose it wouldn't stop? Suppose it had decided to be a self-determined, free-willed universe?

Jock grinned, and started setting controls. His time was coming. It was measurable in minutes, and then in seconds . . . now!

His hand reached for the firing lever (but what was she scared of?), groped, and touched, hesitated, clasped, and pulled.

Grown-up parties at home were fun. But other places, like this one, they were silly. Toby half-woke-up on the way home, enough to realize his Uncle Tim was driving them, and they weren't in their own car. He was sitting on the front seat next to his mother, with his head against her side, and her arm around him. He tried to come all the way awake, to listen to what they were saying, but they weren't talking, so he started to go back to sleep.

Then Uncle Tim said, "For God's sake, Ruth, he's safe, and whatever happened certainly wasn't your fault. He's got enough supplies to hold out till . . ."

"Shh!" his mother said sharply, and then, whispering, "I know."

Now he remembered.

"Mommy . . ."

"Yes, hon?"

"Did Daddy go to the moon all right?"

"Y . . . yes, dear."

Her voice was funny.

"Where is it?"

"Where's what?"

"The moon."

"Oh. We can't see it now, darling. It's around the other side of the earth."

"Well, when is he going to come back?"

Silence.

"Mommy . . . when?"

"As soon as . . . just as soon as he can, darling. Now go to sleep."

And now the moon was up, high in the sky, a gilded football dangling from Somebody's black serge lapel. When she was a little girl, she used to say she loved the man in the moon, and now the man in the moon loved her too, but if she was a little girl still, somebody would tuck her into bed, and pat her head and tell her to go to sleep, and she would sleep as easy, breathe as soft, as Toby did. . . .

But she wasn't a little girl, she was all grown up, and she married the man, the man in the moon, and sleep could come and sleep could go, but sleep could never stay with her while the moonwash swept the window panes.

She stood at the open window and wrote a letter in her mind and sent it up the path of light to the man in the moon. It said:

"Dear Jock: Tim says it wasn't my fault, and I can't explain it even to him. I'm sorry, darling. Please to stay alive till we can get to you. Faithfully yours, Cassandra."

IV

The glasses and ashes and litter and spilled drinks had all been cleared away. The table top gleamed in polished stripes of light and dark, where the light came through the louvered plastic of the wall. The big chairs were empty, waiting, and at each place, arranged with the precision of a formal dinner-setting, was the inevitable pad of yellow paper, two freshly-sharpened pencils, a small neat pile of typed white sheets of paper, a small glass ashtray and a shining empty water glass. Down the center of the table, spaced for comfort, three crystal pitchers of ice and water stood in perfect alignment.

Ruth was the first one there. She stood in front of a chair, fingering the little stack of paper on which someone (Allie? She'd have had to be up early to get it done so quickly) had tabulated the details of yesterday's events. "To refresh your memory," was how they always put it.

She poured a glass of water, and guiltily replaced the pitcher on the exact spot where it had been; lit a cigarette, and stared with dismay at the burnt match marring the cleanliness of the little ashtray; pulled her chair in beneath her and winced at the screech of the wooden leg across the floor.

Get it over with! She picked up the typed pages, and glanced at them. Two at the bottom were headed "Recommendations of U.S. Rocket Corps to Facilitate Construction of KIM-VIII." That could wait. The three top sheets she'd better get through while she was still alone.

She read slowly and carefully, trying to memorize each sentence, so that when the time came to talk, she could think of what happened this way, from outside, instead of remembering how it had been for her.

There was nothing in the report she didn't already know.

Jock Kruger had set out in the KIM-VII at 5:39 P.M., C.S.T., just at sunset. First report after recovery from blackout came at 6:02 plus. First log readings gave no reason to anticipate any difficulty. Subsequent reports and radioed log readings were, for Kruger, unusually terse and formal, and surprisingly infrequent; but earth-to-ship contact at twenty-minute intervals had been acknowledged. No reason to believe Kruger was having trouble at any time during the trip.

At 11:54, an attempt to call the ship went unanswered for 56 seconds. The radioman here described Kruger's voice as "irritable" when the reply finally came, but all he said was, "Sorry. I was firing the first brake." Then a string of figures, and a quick log reading—everything just what you'd expect.

Earth acknowledged, and waited.

Eighteen seconds later:

"Second brake." More figures. Again, everything as it should be. But twenty seconds after that call was completed:

"This is Kruger. Anything wrong with the dope I gave you?"

"Earth to Kruger. Everything okay in our book. Trouble?"

"Track me, boy. I'm off."

"You want a course correction?"

"I can figure it quicker here. I'll keep talking as I go. Stop me if I'm wrong by your book." More figures, and Kruger's calculations coincided perfectly with the swift work done at the base. Both sides came to the same conclusion, and both sides knew what it meant. The man in the beast fired once more, and once again, and made a landing.

There was no reason to believe that either ship or pilot h⌐ l been hurt. There was no way of finding out. By the ʟest calculations, they were five degrees of arc around onto the dark side. And there was no possibility at all, after that second corrective firing that Kruger had enough fuel left to take off again. The last thing Earth had heard, before the edge of the moon cut off Kruger's radio, was:

"Sorry, boys. I guess I fouled up this time. Looks like you'll have to come and . . ."

One by one, they filled the seats: Gordon Kimberly at one end, and the Colonel at the other; Tim O'Heyer to one side of Kimberly, and Ruth at the other; Allie, with her pad and pencil poised, alongside Tim; the Colonel's aide next down the line, with his little silent stenotype in front of him; the Steins across from him, next to Ruth. With a minimum of formality, Kimberly opened the meeting and introduced Col. Swenson.

The Colonel cleared his throat. "I'd like to make something clear," he said. "Right from the start, I want to make this clear. I'm here to help. Not to get in the way. My presence does not indicate any—*criticism* on the part of the Armed Services. We are entirely satisfied with the work you people have been doing." He cleared his throat again, and Kimberly put in:

"You saw our plans, I believe, Colonel. Everything was checked and approved by your outfit ahead of time."

"Exactly. We had no criticism then, and we have none now. The rocket program is what's important. Getting Kruger back is important, not just for ordinary humanitarian reasons—pardon me, Mrs. Kruger, if I'm too blunt —but for the sake of the whole program. Public opinion, for one thing. That's your line, isn't it, Mr. O'Heyer? And then, *we have to find out what happened!*

"I came down here today to offer any help we can give you on the relief ship, and to make a suggestion to facilitate matters."

He paused deliberately this time.

"Go ahead, Colonel," Tim said. "We're listening."

"Briefly, the proposal is that you all accept temporary commissions while the project is going on. Part of that report in front of you embodies the details of the plan. I hope you'll find it acceptable. You all know there is a great deal of—necessary, I'm afraid—red tape, you'd call it, and 'going through channels,' and such in the Services. It makes cooperation between civilian and military groups difficult. If we can all get together as one outfit 'for the duration,' so to speak . . ."

This time nobody jumped into the silence. The Colonel cleared his throat once more.

"Perhaps you'd best read the full report before we discuss it any further. I brought the matter up now just to—to let you know the *attitude* with which we are submitting the proposal to you . . ."

"Thank you, Colonel." O'Heyer saved him. "I've already had a chance to look at the report. Don't know that anyone else has, except of course Miss Madero. But I personally, at least, appreciate your attitude. And I think I can speak for Mr. Kimberly too. . . ."

He looked sideways at his boss; Gordon nodded.

"What I'd like to suggest now," O'Heyer went on, "since I've seen the report already, and I believe everyone else would like to have a chance to bone up some—

perhaps you'd like to have a first-hand look at some of our plant, Colonel? I could take you around a bit. . . . ?"

"Thank you. I would like to." The officer stood up, his gold Rocket Corps uniform blazing in the louvered light. "If I may say so, Mr. O'Heyer, you seem remarkably sensible, for a—well, a publicity man."

"That's all right, Colonel." Tim laughed easily. "I don't even think it's a dirty word. You seem like an all-right guy yourself—for an officer, that is."

They all laughed then, and Tim led the blaze of glory out of the room while the rest of them settled down to studying the R.C. proposals. When they had all finished, Kimberly spoke slowly, voicing the general reaction:

"I hate to admit it, but it makes sense."

"They're being pretty decent about it, aren't they?" Ben said. "Putting it to us as a proposal instead of pulling a lot of weight."

He nodded. "I've had a little contact with this man Swenson before. He's a good man to work with. It . . . makes sense, that's all."

"On paper, anyhow," Sue put in.

"Well, Ruth . . ." the big man turned to her, waiting. "You haven't said anything."

"I . . . it seems all right to me," she said, and added: "Frankly, Gordon, I don't know that I ought to speak at all. I'm not quite sure why I'm here."

Allie looked up sharply, questioning, from her notes; Sue pushed back her chair and half-stood. "My God, you're not going to back out on us now?"

"I . . . look, you all know I didn't do any of the real work on the last one. It was Andy Argent's job, and a good one. I've got Toby to think about, and . . ."

"Kid, we need you," Sue protested. "Argent can't do this one; this is going to be another Three, only more so. Unmanned, remote-control stuff, and no returning atmosphere-landing problems. This is up your alley. It's . . ." She sank back; there was nothing else to say.

"That's true, Ruth." Tim had come back in during the last outburst. Now he sat down. "Speed is what counts, gal. That's why we're letting the gold braid in on the job—we are, aren't we?" Kimberly nodded; Tim went on: "With you on the job, we've got a working team. With somebody new—well, you know what a ruckus we had until Sue got used to Argent's blueprints, and how Ben's pencil notes used to drive Andy wild. And we can't even use him this time. It's not his field. He did do a good job, but we'd have to start in with somebody new all over again . . ." He broke off, and looked at Kimberly.

"I hope you'll decide to work with us, Ruth," he said simply.

"If . . . obviously, if it's the best way to get it done quick, I will," she said. "Twenty-eight hours a day if you like."

Tim grinned. "I guess we can let the braid back in now . . . ?" He got up and went to the door.

Another Three, only more so . . . Sue's words danced in her mind while the Colonel and the Colonel's aide marched in, and took their places, while voices murmured politely, exchanging good will.

Another Three—the first ship she had designed for Kimberly. The ship that made her rich and famous, but that was nothing, because it was the ship that brought Jock to her, that made him write the letter, that made her meet him, that led to the Five and Six and now . . .

"I've got some ideas for a manned ship," he'd written. "If we could get together to discuss it some time . . ."

". . . pleasure to know you'll be working with us, Mrs. Kruger." She shook her head sharply, and located in time and place.

"Thank you, Colonel. I want to do what I can, of course. . . ."

v

James James Morrison's mother put on a golden gown . . .

Toby knew the whole thing, almost, by heart. The little boy in the poem *told* his mother not to go down to the end of town, wherever that was, unless she took him along. And she said she wouldn't, but she put on that golden gown and went, and thought she'd be back in time for tea. Only she wasn't. She never came back at all. *Last seen wandering vaguely . . . King John said he was sorry . . .*

Who's King John? And what time is tea?

Toby sat quietly beside his mother on the front seat of the car, and looked obliquely at the golden uniform she wore, and could not find a way to ask the questions in his mind.

Where was James James's *father?* Why did James James have to be the one to keep his mother from going down to the end of the town?

"Are you in the Army now, Mommy?" he asked.

"Well . . . sort of. But not for long, darling. Just till Daddy comes home."

"When is Daddy coming home?"

"Soon. Soon, I hope. Not too long."

She didn't sound right. Her voice had a cracking sound like Grandma's, and other old ladies. She didn't look right, either, in that golden-gown uniform. When she kissed him goodbye in front of the school, she didn't feel right. She didn't even smell the same as she used to.

" 'Bye, boy. See you tonight," she said—the words she always said, but they sounded different.

" 'Bye." He walked up the driveway and up the front steps and down the corridor and into the pretty-painted room where his teacher was waiting. Miss Callahan was nice. Today she was *too* nice. The other kids teased him, and called him teacher's pet. At lunch time he went back in the room before anybody else did, and made pictures all over the floor with the colored chalk. It was the worst thing he could think of to do. Miss Callahan made him wash it all up, and she wasn't nice any more for the rest of the afternoon.

When he went out front after school, he couldn't see the car anywhere. It was true then. His mother had put on that golden gown, and now she was gone. Then he saw Grandma waving to him out of *her* car, and he remembered Mommy had said Grandma would come and get him. He got in the car, and she grabbed at him like she always did. He pulled away.

"Is Daddy home yet?" he asked.

Grandma started the car. "Not yet," she said, and she was crying. He didn't dare ask about Mommy after that, but she wasn't home when they got there. It was a long time after that till dinner was ready.

She came home for dinner, though.

"You have to allow for the human factor. . . ."

Nobody had said it to her, of course. Nobody would. She wondered how much tougher it made the job for everybody, having her around. She wondered how she'd stay sane, if she didn't have the job to do.

Thank God Toby was in school now! She couldn't do it, if it meant leaving him with someone else all day— even his grandmother. As it was, having the old lady in the house so much was nerve-racking.

I ought to ask her if she'd like to sleep here for a while, Ruth thought, and shivered. Dinner time was enough.

Anyhow, Toby liked having her there, and that's what counted.

I'll have to go in and see his teacher. Tomorrow, she thought. I've got to make time for it tomorrow. Let her know . . . but of course she knew. Jock Kruger's family's affairs were hardly private. Just the same, I better talk to her.

Ruth got out of bed and stood at the window, waiting for the moon. Another ten minutes, fifteen, twenty maybe, and it would edge over the hills on the other side of town. The white hands on the clock said 2:40. She had to get some sleep. She couldn't stand here waiting for the moon. Get to sleep now, before it comes up. That's better. . . .

"Oh, Jock!

" . . . the human factor . . ." They didn't know. She wanted to go tell them all, find somebody right away, and shout it. "It's not his fault. I did it!"

"You're not scared, are you, baby?"

Oh, no! No, no! Don't be silly. Who, me? Just stiff and trembling. The cold, you know . . . ?

Stop that!

She stood at the window, waiting for the moon, the man, the man in the moon.

Human factor . . . well, there wouldn't be a human factor in this one. If she went out to the field on takeoff day and told KIM-VIII she was scared, it wouldn't matter at all.

Thank God I can do something, at least!

Abruptly, she closed the blind, so she wouldn't know when it came, and pulled out the envelope she'd brought home; switched on the bed light, and unfolded the first blueprints.

It was all familiar. Just small changes here and there. Otherwise, it was the Three all over again—the first unmanned ship to be landed successfully on the moon surface. The only important difference was that this one had to have some fancy gadgetry on the landing mech. Stein had given her the orbit calcs today. The rest of the job was hers and Sue's: design and production. Between them, they could do it. What they needed was a goldberg that would take the thing once around low enough to contact Jock, if . . . to contact him, that's all. Then back again, prepared for him to take over the landing by remote, according to instructions, if he wanted to. If he could. If his radio was working. If . . .

Twice around, and then down where they figured he was, if he hadn't tried to bring it down himself.

It was complicated, but only quantitatively. Nothing basically new, or untried. And no *human* factors to be allowed for, once it was off the ground.

She fell asleep, finally, with the light still on, and the blind drawn, and the blueprints spread out on the floor next to the bed.

Every day, she drove him to school, dressed in her golden gown. And every afternoon, he waited, telling himself she was sure to come home.

That was a very silly little poem, and he wasn't three, he was six now.

But it was a long time since Daddy went away.

"I'd rather not," she said stiffly.

"I'm sorry, Ruth. I know—well, I don't know, but I can imagine how you feel. I hate to ask it, but if you can do it at all . . . just be there and look confident, and . . . you know."

Look confident! I couldn't do it for Jock, she thought; why should I do it for *them?* But of course that was silly. They didn't know her the way Jock did. They couldn't read her smiles, or sense a barely present stiffness, or know anything except what she chose to show on the front of her face.

"Look confident? What difference does it make, Tim? If the thing works, they'll all know soon enough. If . . ."

She stopped.

"All right, I'll be blunt. If it doesn't work, it's going to make a hell of a difference what the public feeling was at the time it went off. If we have to try again. If—damn it, you want it straight, all right! If we can't save Jock, we're not going to give up the whole thing! We're not going to let space travel wait another half century while the psychological effects wear off. And *Jock wouldn't want us to!* Don't forget that. It was his dream, too. It was yours, once upon a time. If . . ."

"All *right!*" She was startled by her voice. She was screaming, or almost.

"All right," she said bitterly, more quietly. "If you think I'll be holding up progress for fifty years by not dragging Toby along to a launching, I'll come."

"Oh, Ruth, I'm sorry. No, it's not that important. And I had no business talking that way. But listen, babe, you used to understand this—the way I feel, the way Jock fel—feels. Even a guy like Kimberly. You used to feel it too. Look: the single item of you showing your face at the takeoff doesn't amount to much. Neither does one ounce of fuel. But either one could be the little bit that makes the difference. Kid, we got to put *everything* we've got behind it this time."

"All right," she said again. "I told you I'd come."

"You do understand, don't you?" he pleaded.

"I don't know, Tim. I'm not sure I do. But you're right. I would have, once. Maybe—I don't know. It's different for a woman, I guess. But I'll come. Don't worry about it."

She turned and started out.

"Thanks, Ruth. And I *am* sorry. Uh—want me to come and pick you up?"

She nodded. "Thanks." She was glad she wouldn't have to drive.

VI

He kept waiting for a chance to ask her. He couldn't do it in the house before they left, because right after she told him where they were going, she went to get dressed in her golden uniform, and he had to stay with Grandma all the time.

Then Mr. O'Heyer came with the car, and he couldn't ask because, even though he sat up front with Mommy, Mr. O'Heyer was there too.

When they got to the launching field, there were people around all the time. Once he tried to get her off by himself, but all she did was think he had to go to the bathroom. Then, bit by bit, he didn't *have* to ask, because he could tell from the way they were all talking, and the way the cameras were all pointed at her all the time, like they had been at Daddy the other time.

Then there was the speeches part again, and this time *she* got up and talked, so that settled it.

He was glad he hadn't asked. They probably all thought he knew. Maybe they'd even told him, and he'd forgotten, like he sometimes did. "Mommy," he listened to himself in his mind, "Mommy, are you going to the moon too?" Wouldn't that sound silly!

She'd come back for him, he told himself. The other times, when Daddy went some place—like when they first came here to live, and Daddy went first, then Mommy, and then they came back to get him, and some other time, he didn't remember just what—but when Daddy went away, Mommy always went to stay with him, and then they always came to get him too.

It wasn't any different from Mommy going back to be with Daddy at a party or something, instead of staying in his room to talk to him when she put him to bed. It didn't feel any worse than that, he told himself.

Only he didn't believe himself.

She never did tell me! I wouldn't of forgotten that! She should of told me!

She did not want to make a speech. Nobody had warned her that she would be called upon to make a speech. It was bad enough trying to answer reporters coherently. She stood up and went forward to the microphone dutifully, and shook hands with the President of the United States, and tried to look confident. She opened her mouth and nothing came out.

"Thank you," she said finally, though she didn't know just what for. "You've all been very kind." She turned to the mike, and spoke directly into it. "I feel that a good deal of honor is being accorded me today which is not rightfully mine. We gave ourselves a two-month limit to complete a job, and the fact that it was finished inside of six weeks instead . . ."

She had to stop because everybody was cheering, and they wouldn't have heard her.

". . . that fact is not something for which the designer of a ship can be thanked. The credit is due to all the people at Kimberly who worked so hard, and to the Rocket Corps personnel who helped so much. I think . . ."

This time she paused to find the right words. It had suddenly become very important to level with the crowd, to tell them what she honestly felt.

"I think it is I who should be doing the thanking. I happen to be a designer of rockets, but much more importantly, to me, I am Jock Kruger's wife. So I want to thank everyone who helped . . ."

Grandma's hand tightened around his, and then pulled

away to get a handkerchief, because she was crying. Right up here on the platform! Then he realized what Mommy had just said. She said that being Jock Kruger's wife was more important to her than anything else.

It was funny that Grandma should feel bad about that. Everybody else seemed to think it was a right thing to say, the way they were yelling and clapping and shouting. It occurred to Toby with a small shock of surprise that maybe Grandma sometimes felt bad about things the same way he did.

He was sort of sorry he wouldn't have much chance to find out more about that.

She broke away from the reporters and V.I.P.'s, and went and got Toby, and asked him did he want to look inside the rocket before it left.

He nodded. He was certainly being quiet today. Poor kid—he must be pretty mixed up about the whole thing by now.

She tried to figure out what was going on inside the small brown head, but all she could think of was how much like Jock he looked today.

She took him up the elevator inside the rocket. There wasn't much room to move around, of course, but they'd rigged it so that all the big shots who were there could have a look. She was a little startled to see the President and her mother-in-law come up together in the next elevator, but between trying to answer Toby's questions, and trying to brush off reporters, she didn't have much time to be concerned about such oddities.

She had never seen Toby so intent on anything. He wanted to know *everything*. Where's this, and what's that for? And where are you going to sit, Mommy?

"I'm not, hon. You know that. There isn't room in this rocket for . . ."

"Mrs. Kruger, pardon me, but . . ."

"Just a minute, please."

"Oh, I'm sorry."

"What was it you wanted to know now, Toby?" There were too many people; there was too much talk. She felt slightly dizzy. "Look, hon, I want to go on down." It was hard to talk. She saw Mrs. Kruger on the ramp, and called her, and left Toby with her. Down at the bottom, she saw Sue Stein, and asked her if she'd go take over with Toby and try to answer his questions.

"Sure. Feeling rocky, kid?"

"Kind of." She tried to smile.

"You better go lie down. Maybe Allie can get something for you. I saw her over there. . . ." She waved a vague hand. "You look like hell, kid. Better lie down." Then she rushed off.

He got away from Grandma when Sue Stein came and said Mother wanted her to show him everything. Then he said he was tired and got away from her. He could find his Grandma all right, he said.

He'd found the spot he wanted. He could just about wiggle into it, he thought.

The loudspeaker crackled over her head. Five minutes now.

The other women who'd been fixing their hair and brightening their lipstick snapped their bags shut and took a last look and ran out, to find places where they could see everything. Ruth stretched out on the couch and closed her eyes. Five minutes now, by herself, to get used to the idea that the job was done.

She had done everything she could do, including coming here today. There was nothing further she could do. From now on, or in five minutes' time, it was out of anyone's hands, but—Whose? And Jock's, of course. Once the relief rocket got there, it was up to him.

If it got there.

If he was there for it to get to.

The way they had worked it, there was a chance at least they'd know the answer in an hour's time. If the rocket made its orbit once, and only once, it would mean he was alive and well and in control of his own ship, with the radio working, and . . .

And if it made a second orbit, there was still hope. It

might mean nothing worse than that his radio was out. But that way they would have to wait . . .

God! It could take months, if the calculations as to where he'd come down were not quite right. If . . . *if* a million little things that would make it harder to get the fuel from one rocket to the other.

But if they only saw one orbit . . .

For the first time, she let herself, forced herself to, consider the possibility that Jock was dead. That he would not come back.

He's not dead, she thought. I'd know it if he was. Like I knew something was wrong last time. Like I'd know it now if . . .

"Sixty seconds before zero," said the speaker.

But there is! She sat bolt upright, not tired or dizzy any more. Now she had faced it, she didn't feel confused. There was something . . . something dreadfully wrong. . . .

She ran out, and as she came on to the open field, the speaker was saying, "Fifty-one."

She ran to the edge of the crowd, and couldn't get through, and had to run, keep running, around the edges, to find the aisle between the cords.

Stop it! she screamed but not out loud, because she had to use all her breath for running.

And while she ran, she tried to think.

"Minus forty-seven."

She couldn't make them stop without a reason. They'd think she was hysterical . . .

". . . forty-five . . ."

Maybe she was, at that. Coolly, her mind considered the idea and rejected it. No; there was a problem that hadn't been solved, a question she hadn't answered.

But *what* problem? What . . .

"Minus forty."

She dashed down between the ropes, toward the control booth. The guard stepped forward, then recognized her, and stepped back. The corridor between the packed crowds went on forever.

"Minus thirty-nine . . . eight . . . thirty-seven."

She stopped outside the door of Control, and tried to

think, think, *think* what was it? What could she tell them? How could she convince them? *She* knew, but they'd want to know what, why . . .

You just didn't change plans at a moment like this.

But if they fired the rocket before she figured it out, before she remembered the problem, and then found an answer, it was as good as murdering Jock. They could never get another one up quickly enough if anything went wrong this time.

She pushed open the door.

"Stop!" she said. "Listen, you've got to stop. Wait! There's something . . ."

Tim O'Heyer came and took her arm, and smiled and said something. Something soothing.

"Minus nineteen," somebody said into a microphone, quietly.

She kept trying to explain, and Tim kept talking at her, and when she tried to pull away she realized the hand on her arm wasn't just there to comfort her. He was keeping her from making trouble. He . . .

Oh, God! If there was just some way to make them understand! If she could only remember what was wrong . . .

"Minus three . . . two . . ."

It was no use.

She stopped fighting, caught her breath, stood still, and saw Tim's approving smile, as the word and the flare went off together:

"Mark!"

Then, in a dead calm, she looked around and saw Sue.

"Where's Toby?" she asked.

She was looking in the reserved grandstand seats for Mrs. Kruger, when she heard the crowd sigh, and looked up and saw it happening.

VII

The crash fire did not damage the inside of the rocket at all. The cause of the crash was self-evident, as soon as they found Toby Kruger's body wedged into the empty space between the outer hull of the third stage, and the inner hull of the second.

The headlines were not as bad as might have been expected. Whether it was the tired and unholy calm on Ruth Kruger's face that restrained them, or Tim O'Heyer's emergency-reserve supply of Irish whisky that convinced them, the newsmen took it easy on the story. All America couldn't attend the funeral, but a representative hundred thousand citizens mobbed the streets when the boy was buried; the other hundred and eighty million saw the ceremonies more intimately on their TV sets.

Nobody who heard the quiet words spoken over the fresh grave—a historic piece of poetry to which the author, O'Heyer, could never sign his name—nobody who heard that simple speech remained entirely unmoved. Just where or when or with whom the movement started is still not known; probably it began spontaneously in a thousand different homes during the brief ceremony; maybe O'Heyer had something to do with that part of it, too. Whichever way, the money started coming in, by wire, twenty minutes afterwards; and by the end of the week "Bring Jock Back" was denting more paychecks than the numbers racket and the nylon industry combined.

The KIM-IX was finished in a month. They didn't have Ruth Kruger to design this time, but they didn't need her: the KIM-VIII plans were still good. O'Heyer managed to keep the sleeping-pill story down to a tiny back-page notice in most of the papers, and the funeral was not televised.

Later, they brought back the perfectly preserved, emaciated body of Jock Kruger, and laid him to rest next to his wife and son. He had been a good pilot and an ingenious man. The moon couldn't kill him; it took starvation to do that.

They made an international shrine of the house, and the garden where the three graves lay.

Now they are talking of making an interplanetary shrine of the lonely rocket on the wrong side of the moon.

DEATH CANNOT WITHER

Author's note: I should like to take this opportunity to thank A. J. Budrys for the work he did on this story. The revision and condensation he did on my own rambling earlier draft was so extensive that the story should properly carry a joint byline.

J. M.

EDNA COLBY awoke an hour after dawn, and after no more than three hours fitful sleep. In peignoir and mules she groped to the window, and looked out at her Dutchess County farm —hers and Jack's, she reminded herself dutifully—at orchard and field touched by a winter morning's first light. Just barely winter by the calendar, but winter . . . and Jack's bed beside her own, was still as smooth, as empty, as when she'd made it up the day before.

Separated by an authentic hand-tied rag rug and an Early American maple night-table, the two beds were gray in the light. She stared out the window at the apple trees, at the twisted barren-bare trunks, and whispered, "Like my own heart." She repeated the phrase, tasting each syllable, listening to the sound of a woman bereft. Then she went downstairs, a pink ribbon adding a wistful note to her handsomely cut hair.

She stood before the gleaming stove in the kitchen, making coffee, her eyes unseeing on the golden knotty-pine panelling of the walls. She was thinking over how to phrase her excuses to the farm help when they came to get Jack's instructions for the day. The coffee boiled over before she could decide on the proper wording. She pinched her lips and wiped the stove.

"He might at least have called," she whispered sharply. "The other times, he's at least tried to cover up." She

137

realized suddenly that each of those only suspected other times had this morning become a certainty too long ignored. "I'm losing him," she thought with great intensity; then, in jealous anger: "I've lost him!" And then, finally, in purest rage, she cried out: "No!"

The kitchen door slammed loudly. "Coffee!" Jack's hearty voice cried out on a wave of cold sharp air. "Baby, that smells *good!*"

Before she could react, Jack had crossed the room, embraced her warmly from one side—avoiding the coffee pot in her other hand—and murmured fondly: "Happy anniversary, sweetheart!"

It was, indeed, eight years to the day since the cocktail party at which Edna Arkwright, Assistant Buyer in Ladies' Wear, had met Jack Colby, who was something-or-other on Madison Avenue. She at the age of thirty-five, chic if not specially pretty, trim-figured with the aid of a remarkable new bra, and he of roughly the same age (actually a trifle younger), amiable, friendly, personable in a downy sort of way, and pretty much at loose ends.

Pretty much at loose ends, and perfectly willing to have someone gather them up for him, if that someone showed the slightest tact in the gathering. He seemed to be completely unaware of what perfect raw material he was; content to drift, to meander pleasantly along—in short, to waste himself instead of assuming a settled, solid role in life of the sort for which his background obviously fitted him.

He had left his father's apple-country-squiredom at the usual time of youth to become an officer in either the Army or the Air Force—perhaps they had been one and the same thing at the time; Edna could not get it quite straight—and, after the war, had simply accepted a position in a distant relative's firm.

That was the thing—the thing about him that both attracted and angered Edna Arkwright, with her sense of greater things to be done with one's life, with her code of aspirations that had kept her firmly undistracted, steadfast in pursuit of her destiny. She conveyed to Jack, gradually but unflaggingly, that there was more in him than could ever be realized by a life of effortless progressions toward old age. What was he doing with his life, with himself? To this, of course, Jack had no ready answer.

It was plain to Edna that Jack Colby was not truly at home in the city; however much he might think he liked it, he was growing soft underneath and certainly drinking more than he should. In her complete sincerity of purpose, she saw in his eyes a hint of something that was, if not lost, then misplaced; she taught him to understand that she, of all people, could best remind him where he'd left it.

They were married five months and a few days after the cocktail party and, Jack's father having died and left him everything, went straight home to the ancestral manse in Dutchess County. There they lived comfortably and suitably, once Edna had wiped out the frowsty traces of Mr. Colby, Senior's, last years of bachelor living. There was, of course, a great deal of continuing work for Edna to do, a gradual transformation of both the house and the remainder of the property into a condition appropriate to genteel country living, as distinct from the functional but often starkly unpainted working farm she had found. For Jack, as a sort of gradually diminishing concession to his old habits, there were infrequent trips into the city to tend to the Colby investments and the business requirements of modern fructiculture. Except that, though all of Edna's other concerns prospered as if to prove the rightness of her planning, Jack's trips into town did not diminish as they ought to have. Despite her best efforts, some elusively stubborn streak in him would not relinquish its old ways, even after the passage of eight years.

And now, still circled by his mackinaw-sleeved arm, her neck prickled by the short brown beard he had at her behest grown since their marriage, she realized she had completely forgotten what day it was. Eight years—not long enough, it seemed, and yet perhaps already too long —and Jack had been out since dawn, it developed, doing something special for the occasion, He wanted her to come out with him after breakfast. Something to show her. A surprise . . .

But he didn't immediately say where he'd been till dawn. As if he hadn't even seen the necessity to make up a good story beforehand, and needed time to extemporize one now.

Over breakfast, he told her at last about the late poker game in the city, and losing track of time . . . deciding not to phone and wake her up . . . the slow milk train . . . getting home late, knowing he'd have to be up early . . . napping downstairs on the living room couch so as not to bother her . . . up early, and out . . .

She listened to him with careful gravity, then touched her lips to his forehead and went upstairs to dress.

She dressed in a cold fury, putting on walking shoes and a bright red jacket—it was hunting season—and realized only then that she had forgotten even to order anything special for today's dinner. Well, the woods were full of rabbits. She knew a delightful recipe for rabbit, and it would add something if they shot a couple for themselves.

It was inexcusable to have forgotten, she thought in a sort of additional annoyance; she had always managed things so perfectly. The restoring and remodeling of the old house; the garden club and prize flower growing; urging Jack to write little pieces for the Farm Journal; arranging for Jack to become an advisor on farming and animal husbandry for the local 4-H club; having the house eventually selected for photographing by a national magazine —these gradual shapings of a hundred details toward an enduring whole of gracious living, firmly rooted in all the most admirable attitudes and ideals.

But: the bottle in the toolshed, though they'd agreed with utmost reason that alcohol, for some people, was a disease.

But: the late homecomings, and the excuses, the glib and at first believable phone calls from the city . . . and now not even a phone call.

She hadn't allowed for this continuing goatishness in him. Could it be that her careful management of things was going to be overcome by the very person who was intended to crown them all? Was the intended ideal husband suddenly going to destroy the intended perfection of her life's work as the ideal wife?

Edna Colby saw herself on the brink of disaster, all because Jack, for all his excellent potential, simply did not realize what a difficult thing she was trying to do—how few women had the singleness of purpose successfully to take a man and mold him into everything he should be, and to provide the proper mode of life to set him off, like a perfect work of art in a perfect frame.

There had been a lingering scent of alien perfume in Jack Colby's beard. Edna Colby clenched her fists. "Oh, no," she whispered. "Oh, no, you're not going to lose me now, Jack Colby." And then she turned and brightly went downstairs to look at Jack's surprise.

She found him waiting for her in the yard, gunning the motor of the jeep, a look of arch anticipation on his face. Obviously, he thought he'd gotten away with it again. Obviously, he expected that even if she were somehow suspicious, a little extra devotion on his part would smooth everything over.

She smiled, the perfect picture of the country matron, and got in beside him, sweeping her hands under the backs of her thighs to straighten her skirt. She pushed his hand away impatiently, her irritation breaking through long enough to snap: "Act your ag , Jack!"

The little-boy playfulness flickered in his eyes, and for a moment she saw something else there.

"Really, Jack, didn't you get enough of that in the Air Corps?"

"It was the Army Air Force," Jack said, and put the jeep in gear. After a moment, he forced a rueful smile. By the time they were out of the neatly tended yard, in the center of the trim, freshly-painted outbuildings, she was a country gentlewoman again, and Jack was to all intents and outward purposes her devoted husband.

A two-mile jeep ride through the woods, and another half-mile's walking brought them in sight of a stand of fine young hemlocks. For three years, Jack had been promising her a hedge to shut off the pig-pens from the new sundeck view. Now he wanted only her approval of the trees before he started digging them out to transplant.

A pitchfork and spade, a pile of burlap, and a small hand-truck to take the young trees out to the road were already on the spot. Jack had his lunch—and a hidden pocket flask—along. He figured it would take him till mid-afternoon. Young Harold, the grown son of the farm foreman, already had instructions to get the trenches dug at the new location and come after Jack with the jeep when he was done.

The trees were perfect. Edna said as much with delight even while she smelled again that musky trace of foreign scent in his beard. Later, when he bent over to pick up the rabbits he'd shot for the anniversary stew, she saw a smudge of lipstick on his neck. She had worn none herself that morning. The spot was covered by his jacket collar when she looked for it again. She smiled when he turned to wave goodbye. Her smile, she thought idly as she drove the jeep homeward to cook the special dinner, had been exactly right. He could never have guessed she was lost in contemplation of ways to make him behave from now on.

At four that afternoon, Edna took a spicy-smelling deep-dish pie out of the oven, checked the setting of the small table in front of the fireplace, and started upstairs to bathe and dress. That was when Young Harold came to tell her he'd been looking in the woods for an hour or more, and found no sign of Mr. Colby—nor any trace of work done on the trees. He had brought back with him the spade and pitchfork, the stack of burlap, and—though he did not tell her that at the time—Mr. Colby's red hunting cap.

"He must have walked down into town for some reason," Edna said as casually as she could, remembering the pocket flask. "I guess he'll phone if . . . maybe you'd better go down to the village and look around. He might have tried to phone . . ."

Harold went out, and Edna went upstairs. By the time she was bathed and dressed, and Harold had returned again alone, she was furious. Jack had never done anything quite *this* gauche before.

A half hour later, she was getting worried. By six o'clock

she was sick with fear, and at six-fifteen, she phoned for the police. By seven o'clock, in spite of heavily falling snow, the woods were swarming with volunteer firemen, state troopers, and as many of the older teenage boys as could get loose to join the hunt. Edna answered the troopers' questions with as much presence of mind as she could summon. She told them what he had worn, and that she had brought the gun back herself. Young Harold, she said, had brought back the other equipment. She had gone out with Mr. Colby about half past eight. It might have taken half an hour to reach the site . . . probably less. They had selected the trees to move, had shot two rabbits, and walked up to a ridge with a favorite view before she left. She wasn't sure just what time she got back home; it was before noon. Mr. Colby had expected Young Harold to show up by midafternoon. And that was all she could think of that might help. Perhaps Young Harold could add something.

They had already talked with him. At midnight, they gave up searching until dawn. Next day, descriptions went out on police wires through the state, and across the country. By the end of the second day, the obvious assumption was already accepted, though the search continued: one more unfortunate hunting accident, with the body, somehow hastily disposed of.

There was talk of dragging the old quarry pool, but the township selectmen frowned, pointing out the considerable distance between the hemlock stand and the quarry. They nodded their heads toward the over-night snow thick on the ground, and said: "Likely it'll turn up, somewheres, come Spring thaw."

For Edna, on the week before Christmas, there was shock, and grief shading into sincere loneliness. But it was on the day before Christmas that she broke down, alone in the old house where she had planned the old-fashioned Christmas Eve dinner . . . the roast goose, the pudding, the log in the fireplace.

She fled to New York, to spend Christmas at a hotel. Right after New Year's she returned just long enough to engage a caretaking couple, and to promote Big Harold,

Mr. Vandervardt, Sr., to Farm Manager. Then she packed the few things from the old house she had to have—she could hardly bear to take even necessities with her—and went back to the city. It seemed to her that her own life was as good as finished. How could she ever hope to start, all over again, toward that at best difficult goal of complete happiness?

Still, she had to do something to keep occupied.

Ladies' Wear had no charms for her. She could still remember, quite clearly now that she had to think of it, the tearful interview with Selden's supervisor of personnel when she had, for the second time, been passed over when there had been an opening for a full-fledged Buyer.

"Look, Honey," the no-nonsense, severely tailored executive had said, impregnable behind her desk. "You're not going to stay with us forever."

"Oh, but I am, I am!" Edna had insisted.

"No, you're not. You're not the type. You got all your ideas of what you want out of life in the wrong places, for us. You think Paradise is going to have its floor plan reproduced in Better Homes and Gardens any day now. One of these days you're going to run across some poor defenseless guy whose main attraction is he can give you that kind of life. When that happens, you'll be phfft, out of here so fast you'll break the door down. We've got to promote the people who're going to stay with us."

The memory of that interview was sharp enough so that Edna's first thought of going back was her last.

She settled, finally, on a specialty florist's shop. Somehow, it seemed a logical compromise between her status as a business-woman and the all-too-brief years of her recent past.

Like everything else to which she applied her diligent concern, Edna's shop flourished. She purchased the brownstone building in which it stood, and, allowing for business expansion to the second floor, began remodeling the upper stories as a town house. After the farm, she found a hotel apartment confining.

In the little spare time that remained, she betook herself dutifully, on the advice of friends and doctors, to parties and concerts and dinner engagements; she was introduced to a wide assortment of suitably eligible gentlemen, and was cynically pleased to discover that as a wealthy widow of forty-two she was patently more attractive to the male species than she had been as a bachelor girl of ten years' less. It all confirmed her suspicion that there were two main classes of men; those who were after her money, and those who were after Something Else.

Edna Arkwright had been seduced, once, under a lying promise of marriage, by a plausible gentleman with the wit to see that she could be seduced in no other way. The widowed Edna Colby remembered too well the anguish, the hideous, weeks-long fear afterwards that she might be That Way. She had no compensating memory of pleasure—the gentleman had been plausible, but he had done nothing to dispel the virgin impression that the girls who did It over-rated It in a spiteful effort to make their more strong-minded sisters feel jealous. And as for the rewards of motherhood, didn't she have her own mother's reiterated testimony, day after day through the years? Was the honor of living in the stink of diapers supposed to compensate for the horror of giving birth . . . for the hours on the agonizing rack, for the whole dirty, humiliating mess that was, in fact, a blind animal response to the indiscriminate need of the brute organism indiscriminately to reproduce itself?

"Jack," she had said firmly, and more than once, "that sort of thing may be all right for some people. But you and I are presumably civilized."

There had been times, of course, when some of the bounds of civilization had had to give way. But Edna had always seen to it that even in those moments, it was clearly understood that a certain gentility must be preserved, as it was in everything else. Civilized people could hardly be blamed for the environment of their childhood—there was, indeed, a certain degree of merit in having risen from, for example, a two-room cold water flat on the Lower West Side to a charmingly restored farmhouse in Dutchess County—but it was certainly unthinkable to slip back into those discarded ways once they had been overcome.

So Edna spared very little time on gentlemen who did not remain impersonally friendly. She devoted herself to her shop and her new house with such energy that the one was a going concern and the other a completed work of the decorators' art in very short order. It was only then, with her social habits fixed and her workload diminishing, that Edna Colby had time on her hands.

She was not sure she liked that state of affairs. There were mysterious stirrings somewhere deep within her, and these speedily became a gnawing restlessness that no amount of late reading, exercise, or careful avoidance of afternoon coffee could keep from turning into a chronic insomnia.

There was something missing . . . something . . .

She turned and tossed on her bed at night until dawn came into the windows of her pink bedroom, and when it came it reminded her of Jack. Eventually, she found herself ridden with the notion that Jack was, somewhere, somehow, roisteringly alive.

It was a ridiculous obsession, she knew. But she could not allay it. She understood it to be a symptom of some private turmoil that was shut off from her conscious mind, and it frightened her.

Then spring came. The shop showed a disconcerting tendency to run itself. Daffodils and the first forsythia reminded her of tulip bulbs she wanted to get from the farm. She could have them sent down, of course. . . .

But she wondered if anyone had trimmed the lilac. And the next thought—of apple blossoms—convinced her that she did want some of the dining room pieces from the big house for the duplex. So it came about that on a warm weekend in the middle of May, Edna packed slacks and a nightgown in a hatbox, took the little-used car out of the garage, and drove up along the river to the old farm, unannounced.

She arrived to find the driveway rutted and ungravelled, the lawn ragged, flower borders untended, and the house itself smelling of dust and must. She did not stay overnight, but gave the caretakers two weeks' notice, and drove straight back to town to make arrangements for an indefinitely prolonged absence.

When she returned a week later, she was expected. She had written ahead asking a friend in the Garden Club to engage some help for the work inside the house. She arrived to find the Club ladies had already started work on her flower borders. The man and two women she'd asked for arrived at ten thirty on the dot. One of the women carried a basket ("Miz Barron said from the Garden Club ladies, welcome home") with fresh farm milk and butter, salad vegetables, a still-warm home-baked loaf of bread, and a foil-wrapped roast chicken.

All day, the four of them scrubbed and rubbed and scoured. By evening, the house was clean, and Edna was gloriously tired. She soaked in a hot tub, went to bed, and was asleep before she had time even to think about the sleeplessness of the past four months.

"What a fool I've been!"

She thought it again as she awakened in the morning, with the sun pouring in through the sheer ivory curtains. And then it came to her, unaccountably, that she had once again failed to remember a date. For tomorrow, she realized with a pang, was her wedding anniversary. Was that, she wondered in surprise, could that have been what had brought her back here?

That day she was busy with visits and errands and arrangements. She had dinner out, with the Barrons; when she drove home it was nearly eleven. She went through the big empty house, checking doors and windows, then found herself oddly reluctant to go to bed. It was almost as if she were afraid last night's exhausted peace might not come again.

She went back downstairs in her negligee, made some cocoa, tried to read, and couldn't concentrate. In the end she turned on the television and watched it without interest. At the stroke of midnight, she turned her head and saw Jack sitting in his own favorite chair.

"Jack . . ." Edna whispered. "Oh, Jack, no!"

He sat there, as ruddy and bearded as ever, wearing the clothes he had worn that day five months ago, except for the cap, and his smile was a curious mixture of the tender and the flippant, as though he felt some need to make his first words cheerful. "Happy anniversary, sweetheart," he said, the cheerfulness not quite successful.

"But, Jack—"

"Oh, I'm dead, Edna. We'd better make sure you understand that. Do you?"

She nodded, carefully. "How—have you been, Jack?"

He shrugged. "All right." He seemed listless. That was very little like him. Edna had learned to mistrust him when he acted out of character.

A host of thoughts went through Edna's mind. Suddenly, she was back to her mood of that earlier anniversary. Jack was here—in what way, made no immediate difference—he was here, and she could talk to him, see him, possibly even touch him. It was as if the intervening five months had never been. She wondered if that lipstick smudge might not be still faintly visible on his neck.

All this because of one unguarded tone of voice. But she knew him too well to let it escape her. Knew him too well not to understand what it meant.

"Jack—what happened to you?" The question popped out almost of its own will. She was teeming with things she urgently wanted to know, and she was still too numb to worry about the possibility of bad manners.

With the same forced lightness he had shown before, Jack confirmed her surmises of last December in a few halting sentences. A careless hunter had, indeed, shot the wrong game. Then, finding Jack dead with the bullet through his heart, the killer had chosen discretion before valor or honor. Wrapping the fresh corpse in some of the burlap, he had roped the whole bundle to the hand-truck, carted it cross-country for a quarter mile, and dumped the whole thing into the quarry pool, while the beginnings of the snowfall hid his tracks behind him. From there the hunter had vanished, presumably to his car and back to the city. Jack, in his typically careless way, seemed to bear him no particular ill will.

"The hand-truck!" Edna exclaimed. "My goodness, I forgot all about it and I suppose Young Harold didn't think to mention it, either. No wonder no one could see how your—that is, how he reached the quarry!" Another thought struck her. "But, that's terrible! Now your— That is," she corrected fumblingly, "They won't find you."

It was unthinkable—it was ghastly to know where Jack was, now, and to think that there had been no funeral and no proper interment. Jack . . . at the bottom of the quarry . . . roped to the hand-truck, in the black, frigid water.

"I'll have to tell them immediately. In the morning."

"Darling," Jack said in discomfort, "why should they believe you? How are you going to explain how you can be sure?"

"Why, I'll just . . ." Edna suddenly clapped her hand over her mouth. "Oh, darling, I haven't been *thinking!*" She flew across the room into Jack's lap, to throw her arms around his neck and hug herself to his chest. Only later did she stop to think it was only luck that Jack did, indeed, have the substance to receive her. At the moment, she was too occupied with holding and kissing him, having at last, and so abruptly, fully realized what a remarkable and wonderful thing had happened. "Oh, I'm so glad to see you! You don't know how lonely I've been!"

It was only gradually that she realized Jack was returning her embrace with perfect politeness but with an unmistakable desire to bring it to an end as soon as possible. "I do know, darling," he said uncomfortably. "You see, you're the one who's keeping me here."

She leaned back. "I'm the one who's . . . ?"

"It's—" Jack was plainly embarrassed. "Well, it's hard to explain about how things are. In some ways, it's a great deal like it was before I . . . well, you know. The countryside looks the same—but it's wild . . . there aren't any buildings, or roads, though it's certainly pleasant. There's something very odd about the horizon, too. Sometimes I'm almost sure it's flat; I think I can see a lot farther than I ought to be able too. But it's hard to tell."

"Are there any other people?" Edna asked artlessly. Even in her most distracted moments, she had found long ago, she was able to keep her head about certain things—and the suspicion lurking in the back of her mind had to be satisfied.

"People? Oh, yes, there're quite a few. I can see them, off in the distance." There was a wistful note in his voice. "I'd like to go and talk to them . . . see what they're doing."

"And you can't? Go over to these men . . . and women?" She traced one fingernail through the beard at the base of his jaw, studying his face.

"No, no, I can't. It's because you . . . well, it's because I can't leave the boundaries of the farm—except as far as the quarry, of course." He was fidgeting nervously, she saw; the fingernail was distracting him. Substantial or something a shade less, Jack had kept his old reflexes. She wondered who was keeping them sharp for him, if anyone was.

"And can't these people come to you?"

Jack shook his head. "I think it's part of the rules. Or maybe they just haven't noticed me, yet. Maybe I'm not really one of them—maybe they can't see me. I wonder if you might not be the only person anywhere who knows I exist."

"What about those rules, Jack? Hasn't . . . well, Anyone . . . explained them to you? Didn't Anyone meet you?" Edna settled into a more comfortable position on Jack's lap.

"Oh, no!" Jack said as if repeating the most obvious thing in the world. "The only people who can meet you are people who care for you. They sort of welcome you, I think. I don't know—I'm not sure I know—you seem to just feel the way things are supposed to be—but I think the amount of good that does you depends on how much you can trust your feelings." He shook his head, again, and Edna saw that there was much about his new life that troubled him. She considered that carefully.

"But, my dear, you have a number of relatives . . . there . . . It seems to me your father, at least, or your mother . . . "

"Well, no, sweetheart," Jack said. "You see, they had no warning I was coming. It happened too fast. Unless they were right there on the spot—and, of course, they weren't . . . And now I'm over there without anyone knowing about it, and I don't think they can find out about it, now. You see—" He patted her shoulder clumsily. "I don't think I'm really all the way over there. And that's because if no one knew I needed welcoming there, then it's necessary for someone over here, who loved me, to have said goodbye to me."

"Said goodbye!" Edna recoiled to arms' length, barely retaining her grip around Jack's neck. "I was so lonely I couldn't even stand to live here any longer!"

"Well, yes, sweetheart," Jack said tortuously, gathering her up in his own arms and holding her close. "Yes, of course you were. But couldn't you . . . well . . . let go of me? I am down in that quarry you know"

His choice of words was unfortunate Edna had a sudden graphic image of Jack, and the burlap wrapping, and the hand-truck, and the water, cold and black even this close to summer, and the weeds, and the fish—were there fish in the quarry? Someone might have put minnows in it, mightn't they? She prayed no one had.

She clung to the warm, substantial husband she had here, in the house with her, now.

"And let you wander away? To do I can imagine what?"

Jack winced. "But that's what it's for."

"What?"

"Not—not that—not what you're thinking," he said quickly. "I meant the wandering; the meeting people, talking to them, seeing what they do."

"Jack Colby, I've got you back and I'm not going to let you go."

Jack sighed. "Now, look, Edna," he said, "you can't keep me here against my will."

"You just said I could."

"Oh, you can keep me here around the farm. But you can't make me actually be here in the room with you, and talk to you, unless I help." And as if to prove his point, Jack suddenly seemed a shade less warm, a shade less substantial. His skin took on a curious transparency, and his chest did not seem to move with breath at all. His voice was distant, if rebellious. "If you feel that way about it, I can just make sure you never see me again, even while I'm looking over your shoulder."

"Jack!" Edna wailed. And at this point she was desperate. Her voice changed. "Jack?" Her negligee loosened a little at the shoulders.

"Edna, what in Heaven's name . . . ?" It was there, in Jack's suddenly wide and quite substantial eyes; the roguish gleam, that had twisted her heart bitterly only five short months ago but was her ally now. "Edna?"

"Don't leave me, Jack. Not tonight."

"Well, I'll be—"

Damned?

One night passed after another, and Jack never failed to come to her. Edna Colby blossomed again, and the house and farm had never seemed so prosperously trim, so efficiently run. The Garden Club ladies remarked on the amazing way she had taken hold of herself again. Edna had never been happier. She knew some of them considered it hardly proper for her to be so content so soon, if ever. But she was proper. Not even the most vicious gossips could find anything with which to reproach her. Some of them, she suspected, were keeping close watch on the doors at night, to see if perhaps somebody might not be . . .

But nobody was. . . . Nobody who needed doors

Edna blossomed. She found, now that there was No Danger, that there was a certain element of . . .

Well, she said to herself occasionally with a certain kind of smile, Jack had never again made his ridiculous threat to leave her, had he? As a matter of fact, he seemed rather more . . . satisfied . . . than he had ever been, before.

There was, in fact only one problem. It was small at first, but it could not remain so. The future cannot be disregarded forever . . .

Edna Colby sat in her living-room, and looked around her at the polished wood of the authentic Dutch Colonial furniture, the multi-paned casement windows opening to the rose garden in summer-time, the creamy-yellow walls and deep-napped carpet. She looked at the dying embers in the great stone fire-place.

Last of all she looked into the shining mirror opposite her on the wall.

Edna was now forty-three years old. Jack had been thirty-eight when he . . . died. He had of course not aged visibly in the short time between then and the time when he began appearing to her. From what he said, his body did age somewhat when he materialized—but at nothing like the metabolic rate of her own.

Jack was from long-lived country stock—the kind who looks young at fifty, and feels it still at sixty-five. Edna had once been trim and tiny; during her widowhood, she had begun to think of herself as skinny. The past months had put weight on her for the first time. She looked herself over carefully: *beginning to show her age* was one way to put it; *dumpy* was another.

And the end of summer brought another nagging worry. . . .

It was September before Edna became seriously concerned. Up 'til then she could still remind herself that she was after all, of a certain age.

It was ridiculous. Suddenly peevish, she stood alone before the big mirror and slowly turned from side to side, examining a figure that showed signs of a specialized sort of dumpiness.

It was absolutely ridiculous. Who would have thought of taking Certain Precautions in these circumstances?

She stirred as if waking from a dream and moved slowly toward the sunlit library, where she took the big medical encyclopedia from the shelf, opened it to *Sterility, psychosomatic,* and began reading carefully. When she had finished, she went back and examined her newly-rounded figure in the mirror again.

"Receptive, relaxed attitude." If Jack had seen fit to speak to her about such matters, instead of simply busying himself with what she now saw was desperate enthusiasm, he might have used those words to her. "Banishment of fear-tensions . . ." If she had found the words to tell him how she felt—not now, of course, not now that this awful thing had happened—but last week, last month, yesterday . . . those would have been the words.

For one brief moment, Edna had the feeling of something lost; something that might have been, with just a little more time.

Now her mouth was a hard, narrow line, and the crows' feet stood sharply outlined at the corners of her clenched eyes.

When Jack appeared from behind the turn in the upstairs hall that night, he found Edna waiting in the middle of the bedroom, a carefully packed bag at her feet.

"You brute!" she cried out in a high-pitched voice. "You nasty animal! Get out of my sight!"

Jack stared at her. Then, gradually, the suprise was erased by an expression of dawning relief.

Edna finished: "You just wait 'til I get back!"

The relief disappeared from Jack Colby's face.

Edna had already informed Big Harold that she had been called to the city suddenly for a few days. She left in the car and drove not to New York, but to Boston, where she knew no one and no one knew her. She checked into a hotel and, first thing in the morning, phoned for an appointment with a nationally famous obstetrician.

Doctor Martin's receptionist was quite firm, at first, about there being no time available for the next two weeks. But in this sort of jousting, Edna was in her element. She emerged triumphant from the Battle of the Telephone with an appointment for that afternoon. She spent an edifying morning inspecting the Common, and a few of the more prominent historic landmarks. She made mental notes about other places to see later in the day; she would be interested in attending a talk on Winter Protection, at the Boston Botanical Gardens . . .

She never did get there. The doctor, a cheerful, chubby

type, told her exactly what she had been trying to pretend he would not.

His examination was both thorough and expert despite its speed. Smilingly, he assured her that her symptoms were indeed those of an increased, rather than a diminishing, fertility.

About four months, he thought . . . hard to tell without a definite date . . . and now, if "Mrs. Hartley" was planning to remain in Boston, he could recommend several excellent physicians. Unfortunately, his own time was full right now. . . .

In a dutiful daze, Edna copied down names and addresses. She accepted the little booklet of information he gave her, and murmured what she hoped were appropriate responses at proper intervals. She was halfway out of the consulting room before she thought to ask, "Isn't there some sort of a test, Doctor . . . ?"

"Rabbit test." He smiled, if possible even more heartily than before. "Yes, but hardly necessary at this stage."

"Oh?"

"Of course you can have it if you want it," he said patiently. "Any doctor you decide on will be able to do it for you. . . ."

At Dr. Elliott's, "Mrs. Grahame," having taken thought, insisted on a test. She filled a small sterilized bottle for the nurse, and departed. When she phoned the following day—she had not been able to leave a telephone number, since she was registered at the hotel under her own name—the results were, as she had expected, negative. In the intervening time, instead of visiting Boston's historical or horticultural wonders, she had procured several books of a specialized nature in a small shop on Huntington Avenue, and had perused them thoroughly. By the time she checked out of the hotel that afternoon, Edna Colby, who had looked up psychosomatic sterility in the encyclopedia at home, was now also something of an expert on psychosomatic pregnancy. Enough of an expert, and possessed of enough additional personal knowledge, to wonder a little about how much psychosomasis there might be to some of the case histories detailed in the books.

For four hours she drove carefully and attentively south-bound through moderate traffic; it was not until she found herself approaching the end of the Wilbur Cross Parkway and the beginning of the Merritt, that she realized she had taken the turnoff for New York, rather than staying on Route Six for Dutchess County. That wouldn't help. She was no more prepared for chance meetings with friends and acquaintances than for any immediate steps with Jack.

Accordingly, she left the highway, and headed due south for the Connecticut shore. At some small town whose name she never knew, she found a motel with clean white-painted cabins, and a chintz-curtained dining-room. After a quiet dinner, she walked down to the shore, and sat for a long while in the shelter of a rocky ledge, ignoring the cold and the damp, doing her planning to the rhythm of the white-foam sea.

If she could not hold Jack, without paying this price, then she knew what her choice must be. As the daylight waned, she began to think in cold, carefully thought-out steps without reference to or remembrance of the very longing that had brought her to this situation.

Edna stood up and walked to the edge of the pounding surf, seeing in her mind's eye, instead, the still surface of the old quarry pool. The way was clear to her now: the one and only way.

She shivered abruptly on the cold empty beach.

In the morning, she continued toward New York. She would have liked to go home and close the house properly, collect her belongings, and provide suitable explanations for the neighbors; but she could not risk letting Jack learn her plans. True, he could not leave the farm till she released him—but still, he might think of some-way to upset her program. So she wrote letters instead, and arranged things by phone, telling everyone that urgent business required her to leave immediately. Three days later she embarked on a prolonged tour of South

America, where she thought she would be reasonably safe from chance encounter with anyone she knew.

When she returned to Dutchess County, it was four months, almost to the day, from the time she had left. She did not go to the farm, but took a room at an exceedingly middle-class resort hotel where she knew there was no possibility of meeting somone who knew her as the mistress of Colby Farm. In all probability, anyhow, none of her former friends would have recognized the fat-and-fortyish woman in the ill-fitting clothes, with the brooding face and the too-bright eyes.

She had tried to time her arrival so as not to have too much waiting, but she had not dared stay away too long. As it turned out, she spent almost two weeks in the dingy hotel room, waiting.

When the pains came at last, late one frozen afternoon, Edna bundled up, left the hotel without a word to anyone, and walked the full four miles to her destination, rather than hire a driver who would almost surely remember taking her out to the quarry. She walked haltingly, stopping to rest against trees and rocks for brief moments, then pressing on.

Fear and iron determination drove her. She was in a panic at the coming ordeal; the possibility of death, of some terrible crippling that would leave her alive, but helpless, freezing—with each fresh pain, her heart leaped so that she could hardly breathe.

But she would not give up. Jack had done this. He had returned all her devotion, all her dedication, in this monstrous way, and he would suffer for it.

Sobbing with effort and hysteria, she dragged the burden of her body up through the woods to the quarry's edge. And there, at last, she could stop, fighting for breath between waves of pain.

She swayed on the windrowed stone-chips near the quarry's rim, looking down at the ice below.

Jack was in there, she thought with wooden concentration. Down there, under the ice, wrapped in a rotting shroud.

"Jack," she croaked hoarsely. "Jack, I've got something for you."

As she said the words, the picture of the sodden bundle under the ice returned compellingly to her mind. For a moment, her resolution wavered. For a moment, it seemed easier to give in, to admit that it was her fault much more than Jack's. But she had come this far with immense determination and the courage of a martyr—if she gave in now, she would have wasted it all.

With a moan, she sank to the ground, struggling to arrange her clothes, flayed by the bitter cold. The contractions were nearly continual now. She raised her wristwatch to time them, in automatic accordance with the manuals she had pored over, but her eyes were misted with tears.

The pains were like nothing she had imagined—like nothing her mother had ever succeeded in describing. They were *directional*; great automatic spasms of her lower body that knotted her shoulders and thighs in sympathy, that surged like the sea turned to molten oil, that seemed to be trying to take control of her body away from her brain and relocate it somewhere in the depths of her spinal column.

She reached out frantically for comfort—she clutched the folds of her soft coat; she dug at the unyielding ground. She no longer thought of the danger in childbirth to even a hospitalized woman of her age.

"Jack," she moaned. "Jack."

From somewhere, strong hands were closed on her. "Bear down, sweetheart," the urging voice said; "push, Baby, push. Don't let it break you up. *Push.*"

The knowledge of someone near—she barely recognized the voice as Jack's; the words were only sounds—was enough. One fraction of her panic ebbed away, and her body did the rest of its own accord. She was possessed by a sudden understanding of herself as a function, as a force; as an elemental, marvelously instinctive engine triumphantly meeting a resistance that was all the massive closure of extinction. Meeting it and, with a series of quick surges, suddenly relaxing so that her burden almost seemed to go forth and overcome it of its own volition.

"Take him—take him, Jack, quickly," she moaned. "Take him where he'll be warm, and safe."

She fumbled at her coat to cover herself. She was terribly cold. There was nothing on the ground—nothing that she could see; there was no sound, no cry.

"Jack? Jack—can you still hear me?" She had planned it all so well. Planned it on the basis that she would hate what came out of her torture. Planned it on the basis that it would be torture, planned on the assumption that it would be the best revenge of all to saddle Jack with the brat forever. "Jack—is it a boy? Please . . ."

She raised her arms. Silhouetted against the trees, she dimly made out a patch of russet color from Jack's beard, and the faint vertical tinge of his trousers. Sole shoes scraped very faintly on the stones beside her. And then she heard it—the faraway whimper of life—and she looked at the level of Jack's chest. There was something there . . . something . . . As the cry grew momentarily louder, swelled to a full-throated wail, she saw the boy, wrapped in his father's arms.

"Take good care of him, Jack," she whispered. She pitched herself up to her knees, somehow got to her feet. "I have to go. I'll freeze if I don't." She looked down into the quarry. "Goodbye, Jack. Goodbye—I'll miss you."

"Goodbye, honey," Jack said softly. "I'm sorry about the other girls," he added hurriedly, already gone from sight.

"It was my fault," Edna whispered. There were tears in her eyes as she thought of Jack and the boy, free to roam their world over, now, free to see what lay beyond the wide horizons. She turned sharply on the loose stones.

For one moment, she tried to balance herself. One thought passed through her mind, in a familiar female voice, a voice out of her childhood: "By God, if that little snip puts on any more airs about being too good for me, she's going to hear a thing or two about what it took to bring her here." But it was only a fragment of something —perhaps her first conscious memory, rounding out her days into an ellipse of beginning and of end.

There was a shock.

Edna Colby never knew if her body broke all the way

through the ice to sink into company with that other abandoned shell. . . . She and Jack and the boy had gone to where the world was warm and green.